THE
FISH FLY
LOW

Thanks to Charlie, without whom not

THE
FISH FLY
LOW
Steve May

Methuen Children's Books

First published in Great Britain 1993
by Methuen Children's Books Ltd and Mammoth,
imprints of Reed Consumer Books Ltd
Michelin House, 81 Fulham Road, London SW3 6RB
and Auckland, Melbourne, Singapore and Toronto

Copyright © 1993 Steve May

ISBN 0 416 18836 2

A CIP catalogue record for this title
is available from the British Library

Printed in Great Britain
by Bookcraft Ltd. Midsomer Norton, Nr Bath

Contents

1

Fun and Games

Shirley didn't know what to do with her money. She had trouble adding up the dots on the dice. She moved her little silver boot round the board aimlessly, not counting the squares, not caring where she landed.

'Rent!' screamed Nicola.

'That means you've got to give her some money,' Emmy said, trying to be encouraging.

'All right, I'll pay rent, then.'

Shirley didn't sound encouraged. In fact, she didn't sound interested.

Emmy was helping her as best she could, counting her money, telling her to buy this or not to buy that, warning her when to charge rent. All Shirley did was to throw the dice. She did it quickly, as if she might catch something from the sloppy leather cup. She didn't even look to see what she'd scored.

Nicola asked if Emmy had to go to the toilet with Shirley, too, and wipe her bottom.

So, Emmy stopped helping Shirley for a bit, to see

how she got on on her own. Shirley moved her piece OK, but didn't understand any of the other rules. She didn't pay attention to other people's goes. She missed rent twice from Nicola, who giggled the first time, then jeered. She jeered so long and loud, Emmy was afraid her mum would hear, and come in.

'She missed it, she missed it again, I don't believe it, twice in a row, she missed it! She is dozy.'

It was the first time Nicola and Shirley had met. Nicola was an old friend of Emmy's from Brighton. Shirley was a new friend, a local Grossops girl, with a broad accent, broad features, an old-fashioned perm, and a morose disposition. Nicola was clever, loud, excitable, and very quick to pick on anything she found odd or unusual.

'Isn't she dim?' she insisted, talking to Emmy across Shirley. Shirley sat there with a frumpy expression, as though she couldn't hear what Nicola was saying. This annoyed Emmy. Why didn't she stick up for herself?

'Well, er, just a tad,' replied Emmy in a jokey voice.

They played on.

'How long does it go on for, then?' asked Shirley eventually.

'What?' demanded Emmy, though she knew what Shirley meant.

'The game.'

'Till someone wins, dickhead,' said Nicola. Her voice, as usual, was thick with laughter.

'Oh,' said Shirley.

'Ooh ar,' mimicked Nickie, deepening her voice and trying to make it rasp with a country burr.

This was too much for Emmy. She laughed. Nicola, pleased, laughed too, and said 'ooh, ah' several times more. Shirley looked at Emmy for a moment, then, screwing up her mouth, stared away out of the window.

They never did finish the game. The money got sat on and mixed up, and Nicola bounced her piece round the board so hard all the green houses flew off. For a bit Emmy tried to keep the game going, but that made it boring, like a chore. Then Nicola had a headache, and went upstairs to have a lie down, and that was that.

Emmy packed the game away. Shirley helped as best she could. They didn't speak.

At last, when all the money and cards and pieces were in the box, and the box was under the settee, Shirley said:

'Is that a good game, then?'

Emmy, who was trying to be as nice to Shirley as possible, flared up:

'That depends, doesn't it? Lots of people think it's great, but if you don't like it, then it's not a good game for you, is it?'

Shirley thought about this for some time, while Emmy stared out of the window at the damp countryside. Staring out of the window, she felt rather grown up.

Shirley said:

'You was ashamed of me, wasn't you?'

The 'was', which had never worried Emmy before, now grated.

'Course I wasn't ashamed,' she said. 'Nicola's nice, really she is, but sometimes she gets carried away. She sounds worse than she is. She can't help it.'

'Cos she's so marvellous.'

Shirley said 'marvellous' with a flat, scornful voice, as though she didn't believe there was anything marvellous in the world. Because Grossops was wet, muddy and dreary, Grossops people seemed to assume that the rest of the world was dreary too.

'Yes,' Emmy said, 'she is marvellous, sometimes.'

'Compared to me.'

Shirley always compared everything to herself.

'Everyone's different.' Emmy tried to find something nice to say about Shirley. 'You're much more trusty.'

'What about you?'

'I don't know.'

And she didn't.

She was wondering what Nicola was doing upstairs. Even if she really did have a headache, she'd probably invent some game, lying there on the bed, throwing socks into the bin or guessing what the goldfish would do next. Emmy wanted to go up and see, but she didn't.

Shirley was talking. She spoke, as usual, in an intimate, urgent whisper, as though confessing something earth-shattering, when in fact it was all jumbled,

4

and not very interesting, about her aunt or someone.

Emmy let her talk, half-listening, half-curious about how the story would end, and if the end would have any point. Most of Shirley's stories started from nowhere, ran on for a long time, and then ended without a punch line. This was probably because she wasn't used to talking. Only with Emmy.

'So she goes in the kitchen and tells our Lil, if you don't take that off, I'll give you what for.'

Emmy swallowed a yawn.

The Dugdales had arrived in Grossops late in November, so Emmy had had only three weeks at school before the Christmas holidays. She had been grateful to have Shirley as a guide. That wasn't Shirley's idea, it was Mr Travers', the tutor.

At first, it had worked well.

Shirley was not a popular girl. In fact, she had no friends, unless you count Kathryn, whom everyone hated, and was supposed to smell. Shirley was proud and pleased to be assigned to Emmy, although she wouldn't show it. She did her best to explain how the school worked, but often, when Emmy asked a question, a blank look passed over Shirley's face:

'I don't know. I never thought of that.'

Shirley followed Emmy everywhere, never saying much, never trying to join in with the general chatter, just waiting in the background.

Emmy enjoyed this. She could laugh and joke with other people, but also, if she wanted, she could draw back, and there was Shirley, lonely and secret, ready to give her her full attention. Emmy had always wanted, and never had, a best friend. Shirley was available. Even if Emmy ignored her for hours at a time, she was always there.

But Shirley was possessive.

After a week or so, while Shirley still silently dogged her round the school, Emmy started to get friendly with other girls. Sarah asked her round to stay the night on the second Friday. The following Monday, Shirley cornered Emmy. 'I thought you was *my* friend.'

Emmy said she was.

'Why d'you go off with that Sarah, then?'

Her anger startled Emmy.

'I just went round to stay.'

'You could of stayed with me.'

'You never asked.'

Shirley had no answer for that. The fact was, her mother disliked having other children in the house, and could usually find an excuse not to, even at the last minute, after all the arrangements had been made.

Sarah said some pretty nasty things to Emmy about Shirley, and Emmy couldn't let it go, and said some nasty things about Sarah, so Sarah went huffy, and that friendship never got off the ground.

Gradually, Shirley suggested and persuaded and presumed Emmy into a much narrower routine than Emmy would have chosen for herself. They sat together, ate together, loitered in the same place at break together. They didn't go to any clubs or activities. Emmy had always rather liked hockey, but Shirley found all games boring, so, without really working out why, Emmy started finding it boring too.

Now, when Emmy chatted with other people, Shirley would make her pay, afterwards. Although she was still always there, she wouldn't always talk. She would be off, not-talking for half an hour at a time. Or she would find hurtful things to say. And it worked. Emmy was hurt.

Hurt, too, that in the one activity Shirley did attend, Red Cross, Emmy was excluded. Each week, Emmy said she'd like to try it, how she could go home with Shirley after school, and they could go together: but every time Shirley had an excuse – either there weren't any vacancies, or she wasn't going that week, or there wasn't a meeting.

Emmy smiled. Shirley was in her uniform now, ready for a meeting later on. Nicola, seeing her, had put her hands up: 'It's a fair cop, guv!' And when Emmy started explaining about the Red Cross, and the fake wounds, and the competitions they had, Nicola had thrown her magazine in the air, and cried:

'Wild, man, let's have a bandaging competition – get on down!'

Emmy, remembering, laughed out loud.

Shirley stopped talking, and glared.

'What's up?'

'Nothing. What happened after that?'

Shirley smiled, slowly:

'So she never got no biscuits.'

That must be the end of Shirley's story. Emmy's polite, adult-style duty of listening was done. She said, 'I'm going to see how Nickie is,' and hurried from the room.

2

Nicola

Upstairs, Nicola was on top form, despite her headache. She was mixing some perfume she'd found in
the bathroom with her talc.

'What for?' Emmy asked.

'Because,' said Nicola, 'just *because.*'

The mixture had a fascinating, sticky, bubbly feel,
and a delicious sharp smell.

While she worked, Nicola asked Emmy what the
boys were like in Grossops. This was not something
Emmy had thought about.

'Shirley's brother, he's all right,' she said, for the
sake of something to say.

'How old is he?'

'About nine.'

Nicola burst out laughing

'And he's your boyfriend?'

'Well, if you mean boys like that ... ?'

'What other sort of boys are there?'

'Well, there's Aaron, he lives at the post office, he's
very fat, and he's about thirteen, and you can't

understand a thing he says.'

Nicola hooted with laughter, which made Emmy feel good.

'Then there's Alec, from Windrush Farm, he's about thirteen, and he's very *very* fat, with a fat face, all red ... '

'Like a pig,' added Nicola. And they both laughed again.

Tired of her potions, Nicola turned to the Problem Page in the teenage magazine she'd brought with her. Nicola was very knowing about all the boy-problems and Sex-and-Your-Body questions, as though she'd been through it all twice. Emmy pretended to know enough to get by – which was slightly more than she actually did know – and the pretence gave her a heady, strange feeling. When her mother knocked on the door, she blushed, and felt guilty.

'That poor girl's been on her own down there for half an hour,' said Mrs Dugdale, pointing down through the floorboards. 'She's not that bad, you know. Just a bit of a pudden.'

Nicola laughed.

Emmy tried to stick up for Shirley.

'Don't be so patronising, she's not a pudden, she's a good friend ... '

But Mrs Dugdale interrupted, saying if Shirley was so wonderful, why was Emmy sitting up here with Nicola? Emmy explained that she'd just popped up to see how Nicola was, because Nicola had a headache, and Shirley could have come too, but hadn't wanted to.

Mrs Dugdale at once forgot about Shirley. She felt

Nicola's forehead, and took her pulse. She asked her if she was having a good time. Nicola said, yes, fine. It didn't sound as though she meant it. Mrs Dugdale said there were plenty of things to do 'in the Grossops area'. Emmy asked her what, but the door bell rang. It was Shirley's mum come to fetch her.

Mrs Dugdale made big silent gestures for Emmy to go downstairs to say goodbye. Emmy pretended to cling to the bed, like a convict resisting removal to the scaffold. Nicola laughed. Mrs Dugdale smiled. The bell rang again.

'Go on,' said Mrs Dugdale. 'Otherwise we'll never get rid of her.'

'The Pudden,' said Nicola.

Mrs Dugdale laughed, out loud, which was so unusual recently, it made Emmy's heart flare with surprise and pleasure: and this pleasure over-whelmed the guilt she felt at being mean to Shirley. Anyway, Shirley would make her pay, later, so why not have a laugh now? And so she let herself laugh, loudly: loud enough to be heard downstairs.

That night, while Emmy tried to get to sleep, Nicola insisted on talking.

'Come on, give it a rest,' Emmy pleaded. 'We were up till two last night, I just want to sleep.'

'All right, all right,' giggled Nicola, but within seconds was talking again:

'She's not really your best friend, is she?'

Emmy said nothing.

'I mean, is she the best friend you could find? She's

so thick. And ugly. That fat face, like a big red ... '
Nicola paused, unable to think of anything big
enough and red enough.

Emmy couldn't help a little giggle, though she tried
not to. Shirley did have a big face, and red.

'And she smells,' Nicola went on.

Emmy throttled a laugh.

'She doesn't.'

'She does smell, I smelt her, sort of like manure.'

'That's the horses.'

'See, she does, like a big red horse, she smells. A
big red horse ... '

Emmy burst out laughing, but at the same time her
eyes started to water. Her throat was aching. Soon,
she was sobbing, big heavy sobs. Nicola didn't notice.

'I thought you were laughing,' she said, later,
when Emmy had calmed down a bit. 'I didn't mean
to be horrible.'

'Yes you did, you hate her, she's my best friend,
but you hate her.' Emmy had a tendency to go
babyish when she was upset.

'No, I don't hate Shirley. I don't really know her.
She might be a bit thick, but I'm sure she's all right.
She might wear a uniform – like a traffic warden, and
she might smell a bit, like a big red horse, but I'm
sure ... '

And Emmy was off again, sobbing and laughing,
misery and joy struggling in her heaving chest and
aching throat.

That's the way it always was, with Nickie. She was

so quick, it was like everything was speeded up, colours brighter, laughter louder. And the tears, of course, more painful, when she decided to tease you, or show you up in front of other people.

They'd met in Brighton, because Emmy's dad got a job with the same company as Nickie's. Emmy liked Nicola, at once. Nicola ... well: Nicola never had best friends.

'I have a lot of different friends,' she explained, 'and I like them all, for different reasons, at different times.'

Fair enough: but if it happened to be a time when Nicola was not feeling friendly towards you, watch out! For no reason, without warning, she could turn, and insult, torment, or even worse, ignore you. And then expect you to behave the next day as though nothing had happened.

'I was only joking,' she used to say. 'Can't you take a joke?'

And, the fact was, when you were with Nicola, and Nicola was your friend, and Nicola was in full flow, laughing and making faces and noticing things, it was worth it, even the miserable times, every minute.

Then the Dugdales had to move, again.

3

The Lodge, Slobowen

When Emmy asked her dad why they had to move, *again*, he snapped at her. Later, he said he was sorry, and explained how things had not worked out as well as expected with the job in Brighton. They were making people redundant, and he was one of the unlucky ones.

She asked if they were making Nickie's dad redundant.

He said they were not.

'So they won't be moving, too?'

He laughed, and shook his head.

'Anyway, it's probably the best thing that could have happened.'

Mr Dugdale was an optimist, when he wasn't in one of his moods.

'I've found a much better job, in Grossops. And it shouldn't be too bad for you, either. You never really settled in here, did you?'

What?

'In a way, it's the best thing for you, to go

somewhere else, and make a fresh start. Maybe you can make some proper friends in Grossops.'

Emmy was speechless.

OK, she wasn't deliriously happy in Brighton, but then, who is deliriously happy, except in adverts? Life isn't like that: you can't have everything you want, take the rough with the smooth, good days and bad days – all the guff they tell you in assembly. Now here was her dad making out she was abnormal, because she wasn't skipping round grinning all the time – like it was her fault they had to move.

'Cos it's been a real worry for your mum,' he went on. 'If she felt you were settled, she'd be a lot better in herself.'

'How do you get settled by moving house every five minutes?' Emmy demanded.

He smiled, like that was too hard for a kid to understand the answer, and reached out to stroke her hair. She pulled her head away.

When they got to the new house, Emmy was not impressed. For a start, it wasn't what she'd call a house. It was a squat, grey building, made of big stones, like an electricity sub-station. The rooms were small, two downstairs, two up.

'Is this it?' she asked, after an exploration that took only minutes.

Her father turned on her.

'What do you mean by that?'

'Well,' she faltered, 'it's a bit like somewhere on the way to somewhere else.'

15

Her mother appeared in the doorway. She was pale, and she was still wearing her coat from the journey. She was smiling. She hadn't smiled much, recently, and Emmy's heart lifted.

'That's what it is,' her mum said. 'Somewhere on the way to somewhere else. It's a gatehouse.'

'Lodge,' corrected Mr Dugdale. 'It's where the servants of the big house used to live.'

Emmy's eyes lit up.

'Is there a big house?'

'No, it got pulled down.'

Her mum took a couple of pills, then carried on cleaning and tidying.

'Darling, I think you ought to have a rest,' Mr Dugdale said, putting his arm round his wife's shoulders. She shrugged him away.

'If I have a rest, who's going to get the place sorted out for when the furniture arrives?'

'I will,' he said.

His wife snorted.

'And I'll help,' Emmy added.

'Yes, and I spy pigs landing at Gatwick.'

With which Mrs Dugdale bustled out of the room.

Emmy was annoyed, but her dad shook his head:

'Best leave her to it. It's about the only time she's happy, when she's tidying. Our time'll come when the van arrives. I'm going to really need your help then.'

So, while they waited for the van with their furniture, Emmy and her Dad went and sat on the bench seat built in under the front window. For a while they didn't talk. Elsewhere in the house, Mrs Dugdale was making busy-busy clatterings and bangings and hoovering noises. They were well out of her way.

Emmy asked her dad where his job was. They had driven through Slobowen on the way to the Lodge, and it was tiny, barely bigger than a hamlet, with no businesses that she could see.

'I'm going to be what they call an area rep, so I travel round the whole Wales and West region. The regional office is in Tinderford. That's about ten miles away.'

And so he went on, about the area, and about his job. Emmy edged up closer to him, and he put his arm round her. She wasn't really listening to what he said. He sounded happy, and eager, and that was good enough for her. Lately, he had been pretty moody. On impulse, and maybe in the middle of one of his sentences, she asked if he fancied a game of cards. He looked at her, offended, and shook his head.

They were not normally a card-playing family, but on special occasions, like holidays, she and her dad would play instead of watching TV. It was an odd thing to do, because she didn't really like cards, but it was what they did. And, that morning, when they left the house in Brighton for the last time, she had rescued the cards from one of the big black bin-liners full of things to be thrown away, and packed them carefully in her rucksack (which contained only the most essential items, such as Normous the diminutive bear ... or was he a kangaroo?). In the car, she had asked her dad if he would play. He said, not while he was driving, but he would, if there was a chance, later on.

Well, he'd had his chance, and blown it. Emmy wriggled away from him. She strode out into the back garden, sat down on the low wall that surrounded it, and waited for her dad, or her mum, to come looking for her.

She'd been expecting the new place to be countryside like the pictures in magazines, but Grossops wasn't. There was a hill, which was covered in regimental pine trees, but these were dwarfed by the row of pylons that swept down the hill and passed within fifty yards of the Lodge. Her dad had said the nearest house was a quarter of a mile away, but this was not strictly true. Just over the wall sat a kind of bungalow, which looked as though it had been made with an oversize construction kit. The walls were pebbled brown, but at each corner you could see the big bolts that held it together.

'That's just Mrs Thomas,' her dad had said. 'She's a real old Welsh character.'

As though that made it all right.

'What an eyesore!' Mrs Dugdale had complained.

For once, Emmy found herself agreeing with her mum.

She looked at the pylons, at Mrs Thomas's grotty prefab. Beyond that, was a scrubby, dusty, muddy, churned up sort of area, that looked as though it had been cleared for a housing estate they'd forgotten to build. Emmy felt put out. Surely fathers and husbands should look after their families better than this, and if not, the least they could do was play cards when they'd promised ...

'Pretty, inum?' Mrs Thomas was bending over her compost heap, scraping potato peelings out of her bright red plastic bowl. Emmy had not noticed her creeping across her lawn. She was a short, round woman, with white, freckled skin, and thick spectacles. She wore an apron. She looked just like grannies used to in pictures before nutrition got better. She waved up at the hill with her gloved hand.

'Pretty as a picture,' she said. Her eyes were screwed up shut behind the thick glasses.

'Oh yes,' replied Emmy very politely.

She hummed to herself, to show Mrs Thomas how happy she was. She felt wicked, ungrateful.

Mrs Thomas waved, and waddled back towards her bolt-together bungalow.

Still no sign of Dad, or Mum, wondering where she'd got to.

Emmy unlatched the door of the shed, pulled it open, and went inside. In the shed she found a tin of rusty nails, which might be Roman; and a scythe that probably dated back to when everyone was a peasant and worked on the land. The shed had a little window. Looking out over the scrubland, Emmy pretended she was a settler, fearing Indians, till there was a knocking on the shed door, and with a guilty start she remembered that the Indians were the goodies, so she stopped.

It was Mrs Thomas.

'Little settle-you-in-present,' she murmured, and as though smuggling something naughty and secret, she pressed a hot, metallic, squidgy lump into Emmy's hand.

'Go on, eat it, keep your strength up.'

It was one of those liqueur chocolates people buy at Christmas, supposed to be in the shape of a barrel, but deformed by the heat of Mrs Thomas's apron pocket.

'Thank you very much.'

Emmy made to put the chocolate in safe keeping, but stopped short, realising the mess it would make of her jeans pocket.

'Go on, eat it. Eat drink and be merry!' added Mrs Thomas.

Trying to smile, Emmy peeled the red and gold metal paper away from the soggy chocolate, and pushed it into her mouth.

Satisfied, Mrs Thomas waddled back to the wall, and over it, like a slow-motion hurdler, revealing the tops of her thick pink socks. Emmy, trying to have as little as possible to do with the thing in her mouth, walked casually round behind the shed, and spat it out onto the concrete.

Behind the shed it was like a narrow alley way, and it was very private. A good place to go, and be alone. It was too damp and grotty for adults. The den was already part-furnished: there was a bucket to sit on. So she sat on it, and passed the time by poking at the squidgy chocolate with a stick.

A big vehicle pulled up at the front of the house,

brakes wheezing, wheels scrunching the gravel. The furniture van, must be. Emmy wanted to go and see it, and to help unload, but she stayed put. Surely now her dad would come and fetch her? She rehearsed things to say when he did.

He did not.

Minutes passed, a quarter of an hour, half an hour? She shivered. Her bum was stiff, from sitting on the bucket, but still for another few minutes, she did not move. She could hear the men unloading the furniture. It was like missing something on telly, something you really wanted to see, and all you had to do was switch the set on.

At last, she slipped out from behind the shed, but catching sight of her dad through the kitchen window, she did not run into the house. She sat on the wall again, on the side away from Mrs Thomas. She didn't want another liqueur. The taste of the last one still lingered, hot and heady, in her mouth, like burnt sugar. She pretended not to look towards the house, not to have noticed the van and the men tramping in and out. her Her father couldn't fail to see her.

Something wet snuffled against her leg.

'Tiny, come here!'

Emmy jerked her legs up on to the wall. This did not stop the dog having a last sniff at her knee, big intelligent eyes staring up at her, before it loped off. It was a strange looking animal, as tall as a small pony, but skinny, and covered with greyish black wiry hair.

'Get that thing out of our garden!'

21

Mrs Dugdale had appeared at the bedroom window, baggy-eyed, still in her coat. In her arms was a bundle of dresses. She hated and feared dogs of all shapes and sizes, except Pekinese. Her aunt had had a Peke called Bubbles, and Mrs Dugdale made an exception for them. However, this monster was certainly no Peke.

'Sorry,' called the dog's owner, who was bald but apparently female, and quite young, wearing dirty black raggy clothes over green and pink hooped tights, and clompy boots. She carried a petrol can.

'He's just friendly.'

'I'll give you friendly,' shouted Mrs Dugdale, coughing with outrage.

The bald girl did not argue, but kept on walking, calmly, away towards the woods, with the big dog trotting dutifully a step behind her, head bowed, tail curled under his bottom, as though ashamed of letting her down in public. Emmy, who herself had mixed feelings about dogs, smiled. This dog's eyes had been intelligent, wary, but friendly.

She brightened. She hadn't been allowed to have a pet, well, a dog or a cat, in the last two places, because in Sandwich they'd lived in an upstairs flat, and in Brighton because the traffic was so bad. Her dad had promised to think very seriously about letting her have some kind of animal out here. She thought about having a big hairy dog, that loved her, and did everything she said, and went everywhere with her, and was as gentle as a lamb, until someone tried to hurt her, and then it leapt on them and killed them – well, not kill but held them down until the police came.

She ran back indoors, her heart light. She couldn't imagine what had made her hang about for so long outside.

Her dad was in the kitchen, in the middle of a chaos of boxes and cases and toasters and saucepans. He had found the kettle, and was making a pot of tea. Emmy hugged him.

'It's a lovely little house. Really it is. There's Roman remains in the shed, and it's right in the country like I've always wanted, and Mrs Thomas, she's just like a granny. Thank you very much for moving here for me.'

He laughed, and hugged her back.

'I thought you were going to help.'

'I am, I am, don't worry.'

And she flew off to find something to do.

Mrs Dugdale was all over the place, getting herself into a state, trying to make the men put things in the right rooms. She had started off with a foolproof system, involving sticky labels, but that had quickly broken down.

'It's too small,' she complained. 'There's not enough room for everything. It's like trying to squeeze a quart into a pint pot.'

Emmy found some of her own things, and busied herself arranging them in her new bedroom. Long after the van had gone, she was still absorbed in some old exercise books, from second year juniors, when she was eight. How loopy her writing had been, then! How solemnly she used to try and do the dumb tasks set by Miss Crockett. 'A Day in the Life of a 50p piece.' Wow!

But Miss Crockett had been her favourite teacher of all time: young, fresh-faced, clear-spoken, kind but firm, so sensible not even the wildest, yobbiest kids played up in her class.

For a long painful moment, Emmy found herself aching to be back in Sandwich, aged 8, in Miss Crockett's class, doing soppy things, singing soppy songs. Normous, his head poking out of her rucksack in the corner, looked like he agreed with her.

She slapped the exercise book shut, and tried to focus on the present. There *were* good things about this new place. For a start, pets – maybe. And new people, new friends. And. Maybe Dad would be happier with his new job. And maybe Mum would not be so ill. Maybe.

She slipped out of the room, looking for her mum. She wanted to hug her, and thank her: but Mrs Dugdale was lying on her bed (which was still bare of sheets or duvet), asleep, fitfully. A little trickle of saliva ran down from the corner of her mouth, which was twisted, like she was saying something nasty in a dream.

Emmy didn't hug her, but went downstairs, on tiptoe. Why? The house was so quiet. She peeped into the kitchen. Her dad was sitting stretched out on the kitchen sofa, with a mug of beer in one hand, a fag in the other. His face was pale, almost grey. He did not notice her.

So, she went back up to her bedroom, and sat by the window, with Normous, staring out, and trying to rekindle the eager, happy feeling in her heart, as the light faded over the hill, and night began to whisper against the damp stone walls.

4

Escape Route

By the time school broke up for Christmas, Emmy had got used to the Lodge. OK, anyone could see it was no mansion, but, a house is a house. It's where you live. She didn't exactly like it, but she accepted it.

She also accepted the fact that her mother, despite the pain she often experienced, would be in her oldest dungarees, painting, scraping, cleaning, clearing; that her dad would be plotting and planning extensions and improvements, or battling with the garden, when he wasn't at work; that there was newspaper on the floors, and damp patches on the walls; that bare light bulbs hung by brown cords; that there were flakes of old paint or sawdust in the food.

'We're going to make a home out of this place,' Mrs Dugdale said, grimly.

'If it kills us,' added Mr Dugdale, 'and it probably will.'

And Emmy didn't mind. She got used to mess and

confusion. She tried to keep her own room as neat as possible, and let her parents get on with it. After all, they seemed to be enjoying themselves, in a strange, exhausted, irritable sort of way.

Until Nicola arrived.

Nicola stood in the hallway, and stared about her as if in disbelief.

'Is this it?' she pronounced, with distaste.

'It's not as small as it looks,' Emmy replied.

'Where's the rest of it, then?' And Nicola went round peering under tables and behind chairs.

'House, house, hous-ie hous-ie!' she called, as though looking for a cat.

'Dad's planning an extension,' Emmy said, following her friend as she waltzed about, picking out drawback after shortcoming: structural defects, damp patches, dirty places, ugly corners, spider's webs, naff paper, wormed wood. Sharp-eyed, she missed nothing.

'That's because we're doing it up,' Emmy explained, surprised at the strength of her embarrassment.

'Do it up? If it was a horse they'd shoot it.'

Emmy smiled, but she was not amused. Gradually the Lodge was rebuilt before her eyes, changed from a vague somewhere that was home, to a wreck of a building, unfit for OK people to live in.

'The Lodge, Slobowen,' Nicola kept saying, mock posh, like it was high class dog mess.

Emmy followed Nickie into the kitchen. Through the window, Emmy could see her dad, slowly digging

27

holes in the garden. He was a useless gardener. But he kept on trying. And sometimes, he could be very trying indeed.

The kitchen floor was stone flags, which Nicola was feeling with her fingers, gingerly.

'Scabb-y,' she announced.

'They're over a hundred years old,' Emmy said, feeling stupid.

'It's like living on the pavement.'

'We've got carpets everywhere else.'

'Wow. I suppose the toilet's about four miles out the back, is it?'

'No it's not, we've got a proper toilet, it's upstairs, it's got a seat and a lever thing.'

Nicola was in full flow:

'I suppose you do it here, on the pavement, like dogs, do you? Is there a lamp-post?'

She had moved on to the big walk-in pantry, and was experimenting with the loosely hung door.

'Don't!' cried Emmy again. The door was always falling off at the top, where the hinge screws didn't bite into the rotten wood of the frame. Mrs Dugdale insisted it needed a new frame: but new frames were Mr Dugdale's department, and he was still at the planning stage with the walk-in pantry.

'There's no point getting a new frame if we're going to knock the whole thing out, is there?' he said.

Now, Nicola swung the door once too often, and it lurched over. While Emmy struggled to get it upright again, Nicola drifted over to the window.

'Still digging, is he?' she laughed, seeing Mr Dugdale. 'Better go and say hello.'

'Careful.' Emmy had managed to balance the pantry door somewhere near the vertical.

'Dad's in one of his moods.'

'Oh, great.'

'It's not bad, but he's just a bit irritable.'

'Can't blame him, living here.'

After breakfast, instead of going off to work, he'd wandered out into the garden. Emmy, feeling happy and excited because it was Christmas and the holidays and Nicola was coming, had trotted after him, and started chatting. He had ignored her.

She asked him what was the matter.

He waved his hand, vaguely, as though it was all too much effort to explain, too far beneath him to bother with. Emmy wanted to shake him. Instead, feeling flattened, empty, she went back indoors.

'He's had a bit of a disappointment at work,' Mrs Dugdale explained, on the way to the station to pick up Nicola.

'Well, he shouldn't take it out on us,' Emmy replied.

Now, Mr Dugdale had paused at the end of a row, and was leaning on his spade, shoulders slumped, staring at nothing, like an old man.

'So don't expect him to be too chatty,' warned Emmy.

Nicola snorted.

'My dad doesn't have moods. He's not allowed. My mum, she'd have his guts for garters.'

And pushing open the kitchen door, which scraped on the flags, Nicola strolled across the bumpy grass towards Mr Dugdale.

She didn't waste any time.

'Hello, Mr Dugdale,' she said. 'What a lovely little garden.'

Emmy, following at a distance, silently urged her father to grunt, or turn away, or even say something rude. But to her annoyance, Mr Dugdale actually smiled.

'Wait until I've finished with it,' he said. 'It'll look dreadful.'

Emmy glared at her father. He looked away, hurriedly, as though she had caught him doing something shameful – in this case, talking pleasantly to another human being.

'Found any treasure?' continued Nicola, examining the thick clods of earth.

Mr Dugdale was probably preparing some cheery reply, but he did not get to deliver it. At that moment, his wife erupted from the house, fuming.

It was not a very big row. In fact, it was only a remake of the old pantry door row, with Emmy getting most of the blame this time. But she could take it. Since the move, they'd hardly had a row to speak of. Not like they used to in Brighton, especially after her dad lost his job.

'That was crap,' observed Nicola, after it was all over. 'About naught point one on the Richter scale.'

Mrs Dugdale had gone back to her stepladder, and Mr Dugdale had taken his spade to a far corner of

30

the garden, and was digging again. The girls were standing on the low wall between their garden and Mrs Thomas's. The old lady, in her kitchen as usual, waved. Emmy smiled, although she didn't feel like smiling, and waved back.

'Old bag,' hissed Nicola.

'She's OK,' replied Emmy, and, feeling uncomfortable, sauntered towards the house.

She went indoors, expecting Nicola to come too. But Nicola followed Mr Dugdale down the garden, and soon she was chatting with him, and doing little things to help. Emmy stared out of the window, indignant.

'Nice to see someone being a bit useful,' said Mrs Dugdale, from the top of her ladder.

Emmy went upstairs and sat on her bed, and got out her chocolate box.

This box didn't contain any chocolates: she used it to keep any little trinket or precious thing; photos, badges, jewellery, cards, ribbons, letters.

The box was called 'Val du Lac,' (which her dad told her meant 'Valley of the Lake'), and said 'Chocolatier' (chocolate maker) and this chocolate maker lived in the big picture on the box, which was blue sky and white mountains, and smudgy forests, and the lake; and by the lake a wooden house with whitewashed walls and balconies. It was a good place to be, calm, the air fresh and clean, a place where you couldn't help getting up bright and early in the morning, and looking forward to each day.

Nicola came in, and Emmy slid the box quickly

back under the bed. Nicola noticed, and fetched it out again. She pretended to be sick.

'Slush-y. What on earth's it supposed to be?'

Emmy told her it was Switzerland. Nicola examined the box, carefully.

'No it's not, it says here, "Made in Belgium".'

'All right, it's Belgium.'

'My dear, have you ever been to Belgium?'

Emmy, who had never been abroad at all, did not reply.

For the rest of the day Emmy was a bit cool with Nicola, but very polite, and they played some rather formal, boring games, and went for a very tame walk along one of the lanes into the woods.

But it was good to have her there. You can't stay peeved with Nicola for long. And, as the day passed, Nicola seemed to become accustomed to the Lodge, and it to her. She didn't break anything else, much.

At bedtime, Emmy, almost embarrassed, fetched out some chocolate bars and crisps.

'What's that for?' Nicola asked.

'A midnight feast.'

'What a wild rave!'

But Nicola seemed glad enough of the food. She hadn't been over-impressed with Mrs Dugdale's lentil hotpot that evening. Through a mouthful of Mars, she said:

'That was a weird letter you sent me.'

Emmy's heart jumped. She had pushed this letter out of her mind. Nicola reminded her:

32

'Stuff about missing me, wishing I was here. On and on for pages. Then, as soon as I get here, all you do is mope.'

'Course I'm pleased to see you.'

'Not that I care,' Nicola said, 'because I've got an escape route.'

Emmy asked what she meant.

'My mum said, if things here get too incredibly dreadful, I can ring up and say this code so she knows I want to come home.'

'Why do you need a code?'

'So I don't have to embarrass your mum by saying out loud, "I'm hating it, rescue me".'

'What happens then?'

'My mum rings up your mum, and she dreams up some dopy excuse why I've got to rush back to Brighton, and bang, I'm free again.'

'What's the code?'

'Aha, that'd be telling. But it's nonsense, so if you hear me talking nonsense on the phone to my ma, watch out.'

Emmy asked if it *was* incredibly dreadful at the Lodge.

Nicola thought for a bit.

'No-o. Not incredibly mega dreadful. Not so far. But I tell you one thing: it doesn't seem like Christmas.'

Emmy didn't answer. She realised that her friend was right.

5

The Raid

'Is your dad a hippy?' Nicola asked.

'No.'

'Why doesn't he ever go to work, then?'

'He went today.'

'Not till lunchtime.'

It was Nicola's third day at the Lodge.

'But it seems like a fortnight,' she told Emmy. No wonder: she wouldn't do anything. Emmy suggested a walk. Nicola said no. Emmy suggested a game of catch, or ball. Nicola said no. Emmy even suggested some colouring. Nicola glared at her, as though she was mentally deficient:

'No thank you!'

Yesterday, Shirley had come round. Disastrous, embarrassing: but at least it had broken the monotony. Now, after Mrs Dugdale had turfed them out from in front of the television, they were sitting in the back garden, on the flagstones. Nicola was chipping bits off a snail shell, and asking questions about Mr Dugdale. Emmy was trying to explain that he

34

was still in marketing, but with a different company.

Nicola knew better:

'My dad says your dad gave up marketing, cos he's no good at it, so now he's just a salesman.'

Emmy said he had a much better job now than he had before.

'Oh, no,' replied Nicola, knowingly. 'Selling's much lower than marketing. Especially if you're selling fertilizer.'

'Anyway, he's doing a lot of work on the house, and he wants to start his own business.'

'Next time he gets the sack.'

'He's really good at carpentry and stuff.'

'Yeah, I noticed.'

'He is.' Emmy tried to think of an example of her father's handiwork. 'He made that chair in the bathroom. It's really solid.' Triumphantly, she remembered: 'He made one for your dad.'

'Yes. That was really embarrassing.'

'He's going to make them and sell them,' Emmy continued, her imagination running slightly ahead of her information.

'And then people can throw them away, or put them out in the shed, like my mum did.'

Emmy tried to change the subject. She remembered Nicola helping her father yesterday.

'How about some gardening?'

Nicola shook her head, without looking up.

She was breaking the snail shell into smaller and smaller pieces. The pieces of the snail shell were getting very small indeed. The flagstones were damp, and big. It was like sitting in a cold bath, trapped.

'Come on, Nic, we've got to do something.'

'Why?'

'Cos my mum's going spare every five minutes.'

'I don't know.' Nicola sounded distant, cool. 'I might ring my mum, in a minute.'

'Ring her why?' Emmy asked, aggressive, although she knew this was a reference to the coded SOS phone call home.

'Oh,' said Nicola vaguely, 'I might talk a bit of nonsense.'

'Well,' hissed Emmy, 'I don't know how they'd tell the difference from normal.' And she lashed out with her hand, scattering the neat little pile of snail shell fragments Nicola had been making.

'Ooh, diddums,' Nicola mocked.

Emmy sprang to her feet, and marched off round the back of the shed. She was expecting Nicola to follow. Nicola did not follow. So Emmy had to stand there, in the cold, behind the shed, with nowhere else to go. The Den was a dead end.

When Emmy showed her the Den, yesterday, Nicola had not been impressed.

'What do you do in it?' she asked.

Emmy couldn't think of anything much that she did do behind the shed. It was just her place to go. Maybe that was the good thing about it, that it was a boring, dead-end place, so no-one else wanted to be there.

Now, after the snail-shell row, it seemed a very dead-end place indeed: concrete foundations in damp earth strewn with pine needles, also damp. Only a minute or so after her dramatic exit, and Emmy wanted to go back into the garden. Of course, she couldn't just re-emerge. That would be ridiculous, like an actor getting up and walking off after doing a big death scene. She would have to stay put, at least for ten or fifteen minutes.

While she waited, she tried to think of interesting things to do with her friend. Things to prevent the coded phone call home. If Nicola wasn't already in the house, dialling.

Most of the kind of things you take for granted in the city, like parks and pools and sports centres, were miles away here, and required tedious planning. What was more, transport was a problem: Mr Dugdale was at work during the week, and Mrs Dugdale didn't like to drive too far, because the drugs she took made her drowsy. Not that it mattered, because Nicola hated parks and pools and sports centres. She wouldn't be seen dead on a swing.

Emmy studied the brown, creosoted wood of the shed. She was just wondering whether she'd stayed out of sight long enough, when there was a scrabbling above, and as she turned to see what it was, Nicola thudded down onto the concrete next to her. She was grinning.

'I've been watching you,' she gasped. 'I climbed up on the roof, and I've been watching you moping about in your wonderful "den".'

'How did you get up on the roof?'

'Easy. The water butt. And you said there was only one way in.'

Although she felt stupid, Emmy had to laugh.

'Come on, show me.'

Nicola did. Emmy could get up on to the barrel, but couldn't haul herself up from there onto the roof. Nicola, forgetting to be cool and grown up, did it easily. Then they saw Mrs Dugdale lurking in the kitchen window, so they fled behind the shed, giggling.

After that it was easier to talk. Emmy was frank:

'It's not fair, you saying you're bored. You just don't seem to want to do anything.'

'I do want to do things,' objected Nicola, 'but there's nothing I want to do *here*.'

'What do you want to do, then?'

'Shopping?'

Emmy had to admit, apart from the dingy PO Stores, which sold old sausage rolls and bootlaces, the nearest shops were about a million miles away.

'What else?'

Nicola thought.

'Flicks.'

'There's one in Tinderford.'

'Wow.'

'I'll have a word with my dad ... hey, Nick, what are you doing?'

They had been squatting, backs against the shed, talking in low voices, breathless. For Emmy, this was what dens were all about. But, while they had been talking, Nicola had started to take an interest in one of the planks of the fence, which, if it hadn't been loose before, was certainly loose now.

'I'm only testing it,' Nicola said. 'It could be dangerous.'

She pulled cautiously at the plank, and then harder. Finally, she gave herself more leverage by bracing her feet against the boards on either side of the loose plank. At last it sprang away from the rest of the fence with a loud snap, and cracking.

'Don't!' hissed Emmy, not sure why she had said nothing before to stop her friend. Nicola was on hands and knees, peering through the gap.

'Right. Let's do a raid.'

She tried to wriggle her head and shoulders through the gap. It was too small. So she began to work on the neighbouring plank.

Emmy said:

'There's no need. If you want to get into Mrs Thomas's garden, you can just step over the wall, anywhere. She doesn't mind. She's about a hundred and ninety. You can just walk in.'

'Ve vant ze apples,' said Nicola, still working on the fence. In the middle of Mrs Thomas's garden was a single, small, twisted tree. Its tiny apples had fallen months ago, and were rotting on the ground.

'She said we could have as many as we liked. Just to walk in.'

'Yes,' objected Nicola, 'but then it wouldn't be a raid.'

The second plank came away from the fence. Now the gap was big enough.

'There she is!' hissed Emmy. Mrs Thomas was in her kitchen, moving slowly. They waited until she disappeared.

'Go,' said Nicola, and pushed Emmy through the hole. Emmy scampered, low, to the tree, and grabbed some apples. Nicola stayed behind the fence.

'Look out!'

Mrs Thomas was back in her kitchen. Emmy looked for somewhere to hide. Nowhere. In the kitchen, Mrs Thomas was smiling, and waving to her.

Straightening out of her commando crouch, she gave the old lady a little wave back, then walked casually to the wall, and jumped over. In the den, Nicola was in stitches.

'Fierce, isn't she!'

'I told you, she doesn't mind us coming over. Anyway, I didn't see you doing any raiding.'

Nicola ignored that, and took a bite out of one of the tiny apples. She screwed up her face, spat it out.

'Disgusting!'

Emmy, carefully examining her apple for maggot holes, said:

'I don't know, I quite like them.'

Then they found another snail shell, and this time Emmy joined in its slow destruction.

6

Hot and Cold

When Mrs Dugdale called them in for crumpets and jam, at four, they were laughing, giggling, pushing, jostling.

'So you found something to do?' said Mrs Dugdale, pouring tea.

'This and that,' giggled Nicola.

'This and that,' echoed Emmy. For some reason, the phrase seemed very funny.

'Like what?' demanded her mum.

Nicola put her finger to her lips.

'We can't divulge.'

'It's a non-divulgement situation,' giggled Emmy.

And Mrs Dugdale did not pursue it. She was glad enough to see the girls happy.

Then, Shirley rang.

Emmy took the phone out of the warm kitchen into the cold hall, for some privacy. As Shirley went on about the stables and 'our Lil' and her 'ma and da', Emmy was surprised to discover that all her good, happy feelings had left her. She felt blank, cold, hostile. When she had to, she grunted a reply. At last, Shirley reached a pause.

Emmy said nothing. Not even a grunt. Shirley asked:

'Are you still there?'

Emmy said, just about. She could hardly bring herself to speak.

'What's the matter?' asked Shirley. 'You've been off with me ever since yesterday.'

Emmy let the receiver droop in her hand. As she did it, she felt her father in her, in one of his moods, not bothered to communicate. Every muscle, every angle of her body was identical to his. It was like being possessed. For a moment she imagined him, trapped in the same way by his father, and his father, and his father, the whole family, the whole race, trapped into this 'mood', unable to break out of it ...

'I'm sorry.' Speaking took a big effort. Then, in a rush of warmth, wanting to be friends, wanting everything to be all right, she said she was sorry about the Monopoly game.

Shirley said it wasn't the game that had upset her, it was the way Emmy had walked off and left her, right in the middle of the story she was telling.

'Oh, it was the middle of the story, was it? I thought you'd finished.'

'And then you sat upstairs laughing.'

So she had heard.

'We weren't laughing at you, honest.'

Emmy explained how ashamed she felt, and how she knew what a good friend Shirley was, and how she didn't want to lose her. She surprised herself, how sincere it all came out, because she really hadn't thought about it before.

Shirley then gave her good news: she'd persuaded Mrs Bridle to allow her to have a friend round the day after tomorrow.

'Only one, mind, so no Nicola.'

Emmy, still feeling warm all over, without thinking how she'd arrange it, and anxious to get off the line, said of course, no problem.

'See you then.'

After she put the phone down, she stayed put, on the hall chair. Her mum and Nicola were laughing in the kitchen. She didn't know what they were laughing at. With Nicola there was always something to laugh about.

In contrast, being friendly with Shirley didn't come naturally, it was like doing a Good Deed. But she mustn't think like that. It was unfair, wicked.

She stood up. No point in mentioning the invitation now. Leave it till tomorrow. Or the next day. Hell to pay, Nicola not invited. Forget it.

In the kitchen, her mother was laughing again. Nicola had her hand on Mrs Dugdale's arm. Seeing Emmy, Mrs Dugdale stopped laughing, and pulled a face, as though laughing had hurt her, and got up, and went back to her step-ladder.

That evening, Emmy and Nicola were washing up in the kitchen.

That the girls should wash up had been Mr

Dugdale's idea, so Mrs Dugdale could have a lie down after the evening meal. In practice, it didn't work very well, because Mrs Dugdale could not relax while the girls were doing a chore. She was always checking up on them; and Mr Dugdale tended to follow his wife about, checking that she was relaxing.

Not much relaxing got done.

Emmy was washing, and Nicola was wiping. Emmy was embarrassed, that her friend should be expected to do household chores, and fearful, that it might provoke the coded call home; but she also found Nicola's approach to the job irritating, the way she held the tea towel between thumb and finger, and applied the cloth to the crockery with a feeble, tiny movement.

'It'll take you an hour to do a plate like that,' she said.

'That's right,' Nicola replied. 'And then a grown-up comes and does it for you.'

Emmy said that was all very well, but what happens when there aren't any grown-ups?

'Then forget the washing up.'

Nicola tossed her towel aside.

Emmy bit her lip, and said nothing. They'd done a lot of giggling that afternoon, maybe too much. But Nicola never knew when to stop. She had to keep on and on looking for laughs, even when you were hoarse and exhausted: until, as Mrs Thomas might have said, it would end in tears.

Nicola halted in her search for amusement:

'What have we here?'

On the fridge was an open purse, bulging with notes. She picked it up, and fingered the money.

'Don't!' hissed Emmy. 'That's my mum's!'

Nicola wasn't flustered. She counted the money, casually.

Emmy had seldom seen so much in her mother's purse before. Usually Mrs Dugdale made do with one screwed up five pound note and lots of inconvenient silver and coppers, which she insisted on counting out in shops, holding everyone up.

'There must be hundreds there,' she said.

'Eighty in notes.'

Nicola opened a side flap to see if there was any more.

'I expect it's what my dad gave her. He said he was going to make sure your folks weren't out of pocket feeding me.'

Nicola drew out a ten pound note.

'Do you think she'd miss a tenner?'

Emmy winced.

'That's stealing.'

'Not if it's my dad's money in the first place. Anyway, like you said, your mum's used to getting by on next to nothing. You can tell that from the meals she serves up.'

Emmy made a grab at the note, but Nicola easily held it away from her.

'Ten pounds might nearly be enough to make life interesting.'

'Come on, Nic, you don't need ten pounds.'

Nicola had boasted at length about how much spending money her dad had given her for the holiday, and how if she ran short, there was always her building society account (she'd brought her pass book, which she often examined with great seriousness).

'I don't need it,' said Nicola, 'but I *want* it. Otherwise, I might get drawn to the phone, and start talking nonsense.'

Emmy hesitated. She knew Nicola was trying to wind her up, and she knew she shouldn't react, but she could feel the tears beginning to well up, and an ache at the back of her throat.

'Put it back, please.' Her voice came out weedy, pleading. Just what Nicola wanted. Her face spread into a gloating smile.

'Beg me.'

Emmy was saved further humiliation by the approach of Mrs Dugdale. Both girls heard the sluggish slap-slap of her slippers on the hall lino. Nicola tossed the purse aside. It landed on the fridge, but bounced on to one of the units. The door swung open. Emmy froze in the middle of the flagstone floor. Nicola, eyes modestly downcast, already had her tea towel again, and was drying.

'What are you two up to?' asked Mrs Dugdale. 'I thought I could hear arguing.'

'We're not arguing,' retorted Emmy, 'we're washing up.'

'You mean Nickie's washing up. Goodness knows what you're doing.'

Emmy dawdled to the sink. On the unit, the open purse glared at her, obviously misplaced and tampered with.

The door opened wider. Mr Dugdale edged half into the kitchen. He was smiling a fixed smile, like one he'd prepared earlier.

'What are they up to now?' he asked.

Mrs Dugdale turned on him.

'Why do you always have to keep checking up on me?'

Mr Dugdale protested that he wasn't checking up on his wife, he was checking up on the girls. His wife retorted that there was no need for him to stick his oar in, she could cope with the situation perfectly well, all he was doing was confusing the issue and undermining her authority. Mr Dugdale made strange head movements, inviting his wife to come out of the kitchen, and continue the discussion elsewhere. She said that anything he had to say he could say in front of the children, she wasn't ashamed, she'd done her best for her family.

By now the two girls, heads bowed, were washing and drying very seriously, very carefully removing every spot and drop from the plates and cutlery.

The scope of the row extended to include accusations of lack of respect, lack of understanding, lack of interest, selfishness, and a number of other things.

Eventually, Mr Dugdale withdrew, muttering under his breath. Mrs Dugdale fiddled with some droopy flowers in a jug for a couple of minutes, but her fingers were hasty and clumsy. The vase teetered and clattered to the floor. Mrs Dugdale swore loudly, and slammed out of the kitchen, too.

Nicola crowed with laughter.

'What a row! What a cracker! Much better than that door one. Nine point nine on the Richter scale!'

Emmy did not smile. At least her mum hadn't said anything about the purse. Nor did Emmy. She was pretty sure Nicola had put the money back in it. If she mentioned it, Nicola would keep on and on, winding her up. Emmy wouldn't give her the pleasure.

When they'd finished the washing up, the girls went and watched TV.

'As usual,' yawned Nicola. 'Life's so fascinating in Grossops.'

Emmy couldn't concentrate on the programme, two silly men saying stupid things, with the audience braying and hooting. It wasn't funny. But they called it 'comedy', so everyone laughed. It was like madness, mad people, laughing and laughing till it hurt, for no reason. Of course, there was a Christmas tree. They all had Christmas trees, all the programmes.

The purse kept popping into her head, uncomfortable.

Dad came in, stood in the doorway, stared at the screen for a couple of minutes. He did not laugh.

'Do you want to sit down?' Emmy asked, half rising out of the big armchair that was supposed to be his, although he hardly ever sat with them watching TV. Mr Dugdale shook his head, and turned to go.

Emmy called to him:

48

'Dad, I was wondering, if you were doing anything tomorrow?' As soon as she said it, she knew it was the wrong time.

He paused in the doorway.

'Just struggling to earn a living, as usual. Why?'

Emmy ploughed on:

'Nicola wanted to go to the pictures.'

There was a pause. The mention, and presence of Nicola kept his moodiness in check.

'I suppose it's possible.' His voice was dull.

'I can pay for myself,' volunteered Nic.

Mr Dugdale glared at her.

'There's no need for that.'

He must be in a grade A mood to snap at Nicola.

'It's OK,' said Emmy, 'it doesn't matter. I just thought ... '

'You never think,' he said, and left the room.

Nicola made a face.

'Pig. He can go and wallow in his fertilizer. With ten quid spennies, we can get a taxi, and double popcorn and six slimy hot-dogs.'

Emmy kept herself cool, trying not to rise to the bait.

'Come on, Nic, you put the tenner back, I saw you.'

'Did I?'

Nicola tapped her nose with her finger.

'Come on, seriously, you did put it back, didn't you?'

'Wouldn't you like to know.'

Yes. And there was one easy way to find out.

Emmy jumped up, and ran out of the room. Nicola chased her, caught her in the hall. Emmy struggled, but Nicola wouldn't let her go. Emmy tried to hit her, to scratch her, kick her, but always Nicola had her pinned, and the blows were choked.

'Hit me, hit me, hit me,' cooed Nicola.

Only Emmy's mouth was free, and in her frustration, snarling, she might have bitten her friend, had not Mr Dugdale appeared on the stairs.

He said nothing, but the girls immediately stopped struggling. His face was gloomy. He sort of nodded to them as he walked past towards the front door. There, he took his coat from the hook, and put it on.

'I'm popping out,' he said.

Emmy asked where.

'Where do you think? Buckingham Palace?' snapped her Dad. And then she knew he meant, not Buckingham Palace, but the Drover's Arms, Llandowtid.

'And try not to make too much of a row. Your mum's in bed. She's got her pains again.'

Funny how a big row always made the pain worse.

The door clicked shut, like Mr Dugdale was trying to get away without anyone hearing.

'Great family atmosphere,' Nicola said.

The Landrover roared away.

Emmy darted for the kitchen, again. Again, Nicola, squealing, caught her. Again, struggle as she might, Emmy couldn't break free. But she managed to pull and push her way to the kitchen door, and kick it open.

The purse had gone.

7

Brushing

Mrs Dugdale was sitting up in bed. She looked blotched and ugly. How long had she been calling? Her hair was damp and plastered in a stupid shape like Mr Whippy. Emmy was used to her mother being smart, bright, alert. When the pain got bad, like this, it was as if someone had swapped her for another one, with no batteries. No spark, no warmth.

'I wanted to have a word,' said Mrs Dugdale. Her voice was calm, but weak.

Emmy sat down on the edge of the bed. The bulging purse sat near her, on the bedside cabinet. A bulge as big as the purse ached up in Emmy's throat.

Mrs Dugdale squeezed her hand. 'I wanted to say I was sorry. It isn't your fault, the rowing. Not this time. It's not your dad's fault, either,' she went on. 'He's worried about money and I suppose he's worried about me, and it makes him very short-tempered.'

'We're hard up again, then, are we?' Emmy had

found a brush, and had edged nearer to her mum, and was now trying to section off the wayward strands of hair.

Mrs Dugdale laughed. The laugh made no sound.

'When haven't we been hard up?'

Emmy said nothing. She thought of the purse bulging with banknotes. It did seem odd that her mother should claim poverty with such a fat supply of money. It seemed worse than odd, it seemed a bit dishonest. Her mother yelped as Emmy tugged at a knot of hair.

'Sorry.'

'If you're going to pull like that I'd rather you didn't do it.'

'Honest, I won't hurt you again.'

Emmy smoothed and stroked in silence for a bit. Her mother's cheeks, normally round, rather too round, and red, were pale and stretched across the bones. The top lip stuck forward, like there was a skull trying to get out.

'I thought he had a good job here.'

'That's what he tells people.'

'Is it really fertilizer?'

'Yes. And other farm stuff.'

'That's a bit of a change isn't it?'

He used to be in cakes and biscuits.

Mrs Dugdale nodded.

'And it's what they call commission selling. If he sells, he earns, if he doesn't sell … nothing. He likes it because he can please himself about the hours he works, but of course, if he spends most of his time moping about at home, he won't earn anything at all. It was such a shame him getting the sack from the Brighton job. He was doing so well.'

'He didn't get the sack, did he? I thought he got made redundant.'

'Officially, yes. But there was also what they call a personality clash with his boss.'

And Mrs Dugdale went on talking, about Dad, how he hated having bosses, and doing what he was told; how he was a dreamer, and he wanted to be a carpenter, but all the carpentry he'd ever done was fall-me-down shelves. Emmy, brushing her mum's hair gently, rhythmically, let her talk. On, and on: about past troubles, regrets, new hopes and fears. Emmy didn't listen very carefully. The purse business seemed OK. Her mum would have noticed anything missing, by now, and would have said something.

With that comfortably settled and out the way, Emmy's mind wandered to Christmas, and decorations, and particularly ...

'Are we going to have a Christmas tree this year?'

The words popped out, without waiting for a gap in Mrs Dugdale's chat. At once, Emmy regretted it.

Mrs Dugdale, interrupted at what must have been a crucial point in her story, was bitterly offended.

'Go on,' urged Emmy, 'finish the story, please.'

Mrs Dugdale would not.

'You're obviously not interested.'

For a moment Emmy thought there was going to be a force 9 scene: instead, her mother made herself smile.

'Yes, yes, we can have a tree, if you really want to, a proper one – it's just I can't face the mess they make, in a new place.'

'I'll clear it up.'

'Or we could have a plastic one.'

Emmy bit back her 'oh but mum.'

Mrs Dugdale shook her head.

'I know it doesn't feel like Christmas,' she sighed. 'We will get something. I'll have a word with your dad.'

'When?'

'When we start talking to each other again.'

Emmy told her to keep her head still.

For once, Mrs Dugdale did as she was told. Emmy was gentle with the brush, cradling her mum's head. Mrs Dugdale's eyelids drooped, and she gave out a little sigh of breath, like a baby. Emmy let her head down gently on to the pillow, and turned the light off, and went.

She didn't go back downstairs. She felt too raw to face Nicola. She wanted to be on her own. She felt calm, but funny inside. In her room, she fetched the Val du Lac box out from under the bed, and gazed at the picture.

The magic had gone.

It wasn't Switzerland. It wasn't Belgium. She'd asked her dad. He said they didn't have mountains in Belgium. So it wasn't anywhere. Just a picture, on a box. No one lived there.

Hearing footsteps on the landing, she thrust the box back under the bed. Her hand brushed against

something small and furry and dusty. It was Normous, forgotten where he'd fallen, several days ago.

She didn't pick him up. Things were getting a bit
too much for Normous.

8

Christmas Specials

Next morning, when Emmy came down for breakfast, her parents were sitting together at the kitchen table, in their dressing gowns. They both looked up quickly, and she guessed she was intruding. While she poured out her cereals and milk, they took turns in asking her polite, stilted questions. As soon as she'd left the room they started talking again. Their voices were low, and intense. It was not an argument.

In the front room, she turned the TV up louder than usual.

Some time later, Nicola flopped down next to her on the settee.

'How deadly embarrassing!' she exclaimed. 'I walked in, and there they were snogging each other. My parents haven't kissed each other since I was about five.'

Later still, Mr Dugdale came in. His eyes were red, but he wore a determined smile.

'I've been instructed that we've all got to make a seasonal effort,' he said. 'You've been hanging about

57

too long indoors, so, we're going to go out and do something.'

The girls, eyes fixed on the screen, said nothing.

'It's not as if I've got anything more important to do, so,' he went on, looking at his watch. 'Ready at eleven?'

He waited a couple of moments for a response, then headed for the door.

'Right. If you can't even be bothered to answer me, we won't bother to go.'

Just as he disappeared, Emmy, eyes still on the screen, called: 'Dad? What did you say?'

He bounded to the TV, and switched it off. He looked very angry indeed.

'We're going out,' said Nicola.

'If you can't listen to anything I say – '

'I was listening,' Emmy insisted. 'You said we were going out. Are we going to the pictures?'

For a moment Mr Dugdale mouthed words, as though he hadn't been angry enough yet, and wanted to be angry some more; but at last he managed to reform his features into something less than a scowl.

'Wait and see, ready in twenty minutes.'

And he strode out of the room.

Nicola was suspicious.

'I bet we end up in the park or something. On the swings. Or the Wimpy. What a treat.'

Emmy hung her head, and tied her laces. She knew her father, and Nicola could well be right.

In fact, they did end up in the cinema. And it need not have been as bad as it was. For example, if Mr

58

Dugdale hadn't gone in with them. Or if he'd let them choose what to see. Nicola gawped at the various posters, and pretended to be sick. Emmy made a face. Her dad made a face too, as he surveyed the choices.

'Right,' he said, and strode off to the ticket window.

There were three screens. There was a wicked looking horror film in Studio 1. It was a 15, but the cinema people never bother, so long as you can walk and pay for the ticket.

'I've seen it on video,' Nicola said. 'It's about ten years old.'

Or, there was a sort of comedy about love and stuff on in Studio 2. It was only PG, and Emmy wouldn't have minded seeing it on her own, or with Nicola, but the thought of watching it with her dad was excruciating. Especially after this morning.

In Studio 3, there was the latest American done-for-the-kids holiday blockbuster special, about animals with cartoon add-ons, and a stupid song that had got into the charts.

'I bet I know what we'll end up watching,' Nicola said.

And sure enough, they did.

'What crap,' breathed Nicola, half way through.

'Sure is,' breathed Emmy back.

But in fact, once she got over the initial embarrassment of sitting with her father, in a row that otherwise consisted entirely of sticky, smelly, noisy, stupid five-year-olds, Emmy actually quite enjoyed the film. The song, which came up over and over again, was catchy, and some of the cartoon characters were sweet. There were some sad bits, and a warm, happy ending. She noticed her dad's eyes moist with tears several times, and he had to cough to stop from sobbing when this dog thing got saved from the slave master at the end.

Afterwards, Mr Dugdale was very pleased with himself.

'That was very nice, wasn't it?' he kept saying. 'Really good.' As an afterthought, he went to the counter in the foyer, and came back with two bags.

'For you two, for being so good,' he said, giving one bag to each of them. Emmy opened her bag. Inside was a green and orange soft toy, a Puddleflump, or something, merchandised from the film.

Nicola, peering into her bag, made discreet sick gestures. Emmy tried to say thank you, but it didn't come out very grateful.

'I'll take it back, if you don't like it,' cried her father, cheerily. He was sure she liked it really. She liked all soft toys, didn't she? Like that stupid kangaroo.

'It's just what I always wanted,' lisped Nicola.

If he noticed the sarcasm, Mr Dugdale did not show it.

'Now, I'm in a bit of a quandary,' he went on. 'I've got a few boring, business type things to do – '

'That's OK,' said Emmy quickly. 'We'll be fine on our own.'

'Only for an hour, say?' Mr Dugdale appealed to Nicola, as though hers was the final decision.

'Yes, I'm sure we'll find something to do.'

And they did. For a start, Nicola took her Puddleflump back to the counter, and got a refund.

'What if he asks where it is?' Emmy said.

'I'll think of something,' replied Nicola, sinking her teeth into the fudge she'd bought with the money.

Then they went and looked round the shops.

Nicola strutted about, picking things up and dropping them carelessly. Emmy, scared of being told off, tidied up after her.

'That's what the menials are for,' said Nicola grandly. 'Now, I want something for a tenner.'

'You won't get much then,' Emmy replied. But the meaning of the remark was not lost on her.

Nicola drew a ten pound note from her purse. Of course, there was no way of telling if this was *the* note.

'Such a lovely crisp new ten pound note, I've just got to spend it, it's burning a hole in my pocket.'

Emmy said nothing. Nicola started talking to the banknote.

'I suppose I could put you back, cos her mum's so thick she hasn't noticed you've gone, yet, but then, she's *so* thick, she probably won't notice, ever, so I might as well keep you for ever.'

Still Emmy said nothing. Nicola went on talking: 'But I don't want to keep you for ever. I know you love me but I want to spend you.' Nicola pretended to be tormented by the choice, like a soap star at the break. 'No, I can't resist it, I've got to spend you, you're so lovely and crinkly.'

Which was too much for Emmy.

'Do what you like with it, you silly cow,' she said, spitting with anger. 'You think you're so funny, you're just childish. And you can ring home, and you can talk your nonsense, I don't care. I'll be glad to see the back of you. I didn't want you here in the first place.'

And she stomped on ahead.

Nicola flushed, and tossed her head, but she did not reply, and she did not mention the ten pound note again. However, every time they passed a phone box, she paused, and looked in her purse, as if for change.

When Mr Dugdale met them, he did not notice any tension. His business seemed to have gone well. His breath smelt of beer.

'We had a great time,' he told his wife that evening. 'Didn't we girls?'

They nodded without enthusiasm.

'Looks like it,' said Mrs Dugdale, who had noticed that the girls were hardly speaking to each other.

'And we got another Member of the Family. Show your mum what we got,' Mr Dugdale urged his daughter.

Reluctantly, she fetched the bag and offered it to her mother. Emmy dreaded her reaction.

Mrs Dugdale opened the bag, took out the wretched green and orange floppy thing, and looked at it. One of her eyebrows rose, and the corner of her mouth twisted.

'Nice, isn't he?' said Mr Dugdale. 'I got one for Nicola too.'

'Mine's very similar,' Nicola said, 'but more turquoise than green.'

Suppressing a smile, Mrs Dugdale turned to Emmy. 'What's his name?'

Emmy grinned with relief. Her mum was going to be kind.

'He hasn't got a name, yet,' she said.

'Mine's called Grotty,' volunteered Nicola, but no one took any notice. Emmy carefully put the creature back in its bag, and took it upstairs.

Things were looking up. Her mother must be in a very good mood, not to take the chance of inflicting pain on Mr Dugdale. And if she was in such a good mood, she could not have missed the ten pounds from her purse. In fact, it was a pretty safe bet that Nicola hadn't taken the money at all. She was just pretending she had, to wind Emmy up. What's more, Emmy had taken a stand, and given Nicola a piece of her mind, and Nicola hadn't phoned home.

Emmy suddenly felt happy again. She bounded down the stairs. She was going to start talking to Nicola again, straight away. As she pushed her way back into the kitchen, her mother was saying:

'Yes, but what about the tree?'

9

Tops

Mr Dugdale smote his forehead.

'Oh no! I forgot.'

'What tree?' asked Emmy.

'Your father was supposed to be buying a tree today. That's what we decided.'

Emmy looked to her dad. Surely he hadn't forgotten, really?

'We aren't having a tree this year,' remarked Nicola. 'Mum asked, but I said not to bother. I'd rather have the money.'

'Yes,' said Mr Dugdale, his mouth down-turned. 'I think that's a very sensible attitude.'

'Only because you forgot to get one.'

Mr Dugdale jumped up, crowing.

'Fooled you, fooled you.'

The tree was rather a strange shape.

'It's called a top.'

And while Mr Dugdale and Emmy struggled to get it wedged into a bucket, he explained what that meant.

'It's not a whole tree, it's just the tip. They cut the whole tree down, and use the big bit for telegraph poles, and things.'

Emmy thought this an excellent idea, from a Green point of view. Nicola sniffed, and crossed her legs, and flicked a few more pages in her magazine.

Eventually, they got the tree more or less upright, and Emmy went looking for decorations. She found one smallish box of tinsel and baubles.

'I expect the rest got thrown out in the move,' her mum said. She was up to her elbows in sticky mixture, pounding it with a wooden spoon in a big plastic bowl. 'Is it a nice tree?'

'Yes. Come and have a look. It took us ages to get it in the bucket.'

Mrs Dugdale promised she would come and see it, in a minute, but at the moment she was busy.

'What bucket did you use?' she added, but Emmy had gone.

Mr Dugdale had gone to pour himself a celebration drink. Nicola still sat with her magazine.

'Come on, Nic,' urged Emmy. 'Come and give us a hand.'

Nicola smiled. 'I'm a bit old for Father Christmas.'

'Come on, I know I was nasty when we were out, but I'm sorry, OK? I've said I'm sorry. What more can I do?'

Nicola merely raised her eyebrows, shrugged her shoulders, and turned her attention back to her magazine. Emmy bit back her irritation, and started to decorate the tree, on her own.

This wasn't easy. It wasn't a trim, neat tree. It was damp, and big, and misshapen. The lower needles were brown and muddy. It was like having a bit of the forest in the room with you. The tree seemed to swallow up the tinsel. The crackers looked silly, like frilly knickers on a weightlifter. Emmy, chirpy at first, got more and more irritated, arranging and rearranging, never satisfied. Nicola's occasional sarcastic comments didn't help.

Mr Dugdale came in, proudly leading his wife by the elbow.

He gestured towards the tree.

'Da-da!' he said.

'I haven't finished yet,' Emmy said hastily. 'We need more tinsel. Or I could make lanterns and things.'

Nicola snorted.

'Then we'll all sing away in a manger.'

Mrs Dugdale tried to smile. She couldn't.

'What do you think?' said Mr Dugdale.

'It's horrible. How much did they sting you for it?'

Mr Dugdale explained that the tree had hardly cost him anything. He'd met this man in Tinderford –

'Not in the pub by any chance?' interrupted his wife.

Mr Dugdale nodded, and pressed on:

'And he had a whole truck load, and he was desperate to get rid of them.'

'I bet he was,' said Mrs Dugdale. 'He must have seen you coming. It's not like a real Christmas tree at all.'

'It is a real tree,' urged Emmy, remembering what

her Dad had said. 'It's not a silly little tree that's been cut down and won't be any use to anyone, it's the top off one of the big trees they use for logs and telegraph poles, so it's not wasteful.'

'That's as may be,' said Mrs Dugdale. 'But I'm not having it in this house.'

Mr Dugdale had already picked the tree up, and was manoeuvring it towards the door.

'Watch what you're doing!' exclaimed his wife.

Mr Dugdale, in knocking the tree against the door jamb, had scattered several hundred brownish needles over the carpet. Mrs Dugdale, crouching down, picked at the needles with her fingers. 'It's hell getting them up. They block the Hoover. It must be one of last year's.'

Emmy tried to think of some way of saving the tree, and her dad's self respect.

'Can't we plant it in the garden?'

'Don't be so stupid,' snapped Mrs Dugdale. 'It wouldn't grow. It's dead. It's no use to anyone, a complete waste of space.'

Mr Dugdale said:

'Your mum's right. I was stupid. Trying to save money. I'll go and get a proper one tomorrow.'

Mrs Dugdale said she doubted there'd be any proper ones left in the shops, and if he'd wanted to save money, he'd have done better not buying hideous Flumpo dolls that no one wanted.

Mr Dugdale's head sank lower as he struggled through the doorway. Emmy was indignant, hot with love and pity.

'I did want it, it's not hideous, it's nice!'

'Don't be ridiculous,' snapped her mother, scornfully. 'It's disgusting, and you know it.'

Emmy burst into tears, and ran from the room, and threw herself on the living room carpet.

The carpet was horrible, all doggy and stained, left over by the last people. The rough feel of it on her cheek made her wail even more. She hadn't had a tantrum for some months, and her body had grown in the meantime.

She felt big and 'unnecessary', as her gran would have said. It was like when she used to wear mum's shoes for dressing up. The Emmy having the tantrum was small, hot and bothered, hardly more than a baby; Emmy, the body, belonged to a young adult, and didn't particularly enjoy being hurled about on this dirty carpet. She was already wishing she hadn't lost control, but it was too late now. Like charging off behind the shed, yesterday. Once you've started, you've got to finish. You can't call it off half way through.

The door, which she'd slammed behind her, swung open. Through her tears, Emmy saw her mother standing in the doorway, her dungarees hanging by one strap. Her hair was wild, her face red. Emmy howled louder, kicking her feet out backwards.

Her mother was in a rage. She spluttered, she yelled. What she yelled didn't always make sense. It had to do with Emmy being like a baby, and wishing she had a daughter like Nicola, not because she was bright, but because she was so much more mature.

'You can talk to her, like an adult, not like this.'

Emmy, devastated, cast about for something to hit at Nicola with. She started screaming, too. What she screamed didn't always make sense, either, half the syllables swallowed in sobs.

'She's a liar, she makes it up, she just copies her dad, and mum, what they say, she's laughing at you, and she took, and she said … the house … was scabby!'

'It is!' Mrs Dugdale snarled. Her eyes were hot with fury, and pain. She laughed, and coughed, her words choked into spit on her lips. Emmy, frightened, stopped whinging and kicking her legs. Why had she argued? Why hadn't she just said yes and no and let her mother have her way?

Mr Dugdale came in. He was wearing his wellingtons. He must have just disposed of the tree. Emmy hoped her mum wouldn't notice the mud on his boots. Mrs Dugdale was leaning against the door, her head hunched lower than her shoulders, quivering, like someone who's just been shot in a film. Emmy wanted to say sorry, to be hugged, for everything to be all right: but she knew it wasn't all right.

Mr Dugdale gave her a hateful look, and went to his wife, and put his arms round her. At first she pushed him away, but then allowed her head to sink onto his chest.

'That girl,' she said, 'I just don't know. What have we done wrong?'

She was still complaining as Mr Dugdale led her out of the room.

Emmy waited.

Silence.

She lay very still. She no longer kicked her legs, or sobbed, or thought. As her tears cooled and dried her face to a mask, she picked at something stuck to the carpet. It had probably been there years, and it was probably something really disgusting, but she kept on picking at it.

Much later, although it was still quite early, she dragged herself to her bedroom. The Puddleflump bag was there, on her desk, all cheap and smug and hateful. She tried to screw it up, but the Puddleflump inside was too spongy, so she just thrust it as deep as she could into her wicker frog-shaped waste basket. Then she lay down in the dark, with the curtains open, and her clothes on, under the shiny quilt, on top of the duvet. Reaching down, she felt Normous, dusty, under the bed.

Later still, Nicola came in, and switched the light on. As usual, she spent some time arranging her hair and moisturising her face. Emmy, exposed in her misery, managed to stumble herself undressed and properly into bed.

Emmy wasn't quite sure if they were on speaking terms or not, and was wearily preparing herself for more nastiness; but Nicola was surprisingly cheerful. She'd probably phoned home and knew she would soon be rescued. Lucky her. Emmy was too low to care. Nicola chatted on, about this and that, as though nothing out of the ordinary had happened, and without seeming to expect replies. That was a relief.

'They're such a laugh, your folks,' she said. 'The way they get worked up over everything. Funny thing is, you can see it coming a mile off. Your dad, he's a darling really, but she just hasn't got a clue how to handle him. And he hasn't got a clue how to handle her. And then you put your two penn'orth in, and you're all at it, hammer and tongs. Amazing. I wouldn't stand for it.'

Despite the light, Emmy was half asleep, dreaming of having a baby of her own, like the one in the film, and looking after it, and she was always kind to it, and never said hateful things.

'But what if it's orange and green?' crowed Nicola, who wore a mask like a devil, but the good warm feelings were too strong, Emmy was determined to keep the dream happy, and –

She woke up, cold, startled. The room was now dark.

Something had woken her: a shout? Nicola was snuffling lightly in her sleep.

Was the shout in the dream?

She listened to the creaking silence of the house. She could make out the low voice of her father. It was coming from downstairs.

There was nothing to worry about. The row was over, maybe the tantrum had been a good thing, bringing her mum and dad closer, united against her. In the morning, things would be OK.

She was warm, and she had a baby ... well, only in the dream, but she could drift easily back into that warm lovely ...

Another shout. This time she heard it clearly. It was mum.

'You took it out of my purse, didn't you?'

It was like a knife slicing through Emmy's heart. She was wide awake. Her mum shouted again, in a strange voice, almost like a man:

'You took it, didn't you? And you spent it on drink, didn't you? Didn't you?'

10

Counting

For some time, Emmy stood outside the kitchen door, her hand on the handle, not daring to open it. Inside the kitchen, her mother had progressed from ranting to sobbing. Mr Dugdale didn't say much, until for the ninetieth time his wife said why hadn't he asked her for money if he wanted to go and have a drink: and then he bellowed that he hadn't touched her effing money, and something slammed down on the floor.

The door flew open, Emmy shrank back. Mr Dugdale shot out, with his wife, now pleading, in pursuit.

'Please, don't, I didn't mean it, take it all, I don't care.'

They saw Emmy, and stopped. They seemed surprised to be reminded that they had a daughter.

Mr Dugdale turned away, and went into the front room. Mrs Dugdale twisted her blotchy and bloated face into a smile:

'Couldn't you sleep, darling?'

The purse lay open on the kitchen floor, tossed aside.

'Better go back to bed,' said Mrs Dugdale, moving away. 'Come and see you in a minute.'

Emmy did not do as she was told. She followed her mother through into the front room. Mr Dugdale had pulled the curtains open, and was leaning on his elbows on the window sill, forehead against the glass, staring out into darkness. Mrs Dugdale perched herself on a chair, gulping like a fish.

'There's nothing you can do,' she said to Emmy.

'Go back to bed,' said her dad.

Emmy, inside, was hurt, desperate, but part of her floated above all that, calm, calculating. She saw her parents as she had never seen them before: two human beings, children like her, full of love and hatred, desires and hopes and frustration. It would be pointless for her, too, to lose control. She must remain calm, and manipulate the situation as best she could.

'Dad didn't take that money,' she said. 'I did.'

The 'I' jumped into her head and out of her mouth just as she was about to say 'Nicola'. If she said 'Nicola', that would make things worse. Accusations, counter-accusations, complications. She must be brave, and take it on herself.

'While we were washing up the other night. The purse was open. The money was bulging out of it. It was a stupid, wrong thing to do.'

Mrs Dugdale shook her head, crying again, sobbing out something about this being the end, Emmy

74

trying to ruin her marriage, cos Emmy had always liked her dad better than her, she just wanted her out of the way, they'd planned it all.

Mr Dugdale stared at his daughter, keenly.

'*You* took it, did you?'

Emmy took a deep breath.

'Yes.'

Then her father smiled.

'Where is it, then?'

Emmy was ready to be shouted at, threatened, punished, even slapped; she was not prepared for this question. She could think of nothing to say.

'Did it vanish itself away?' asked her dad, not unkindly.

'I spent it.'

This made Mrs Dugdale cry harder; but her husband laughed.

'On what did you spend it?'

'Today, in Tinderford – on the machines.'

She stopped. He was looking past her. Emmy turned.

Nicola, hands behind her back, stood against the door jamb, yawning far more than was necessary.

Mrs Dugdale tried her smile again.

'Just a silly row, Nickie,' she said. 'No need for you to worry.'

Mr Dugdale said: 'Unless you happen to know anything about a ten pound note?'

'Don't try and involve her!' exclaimed his wife.

'Lost some money, have you?' asked Nicola, calmly.

'Yes.' Mrs Dugdale was passing into her world-weary, hard-done-by phase. 'But let's all just forget about it, shall we? Let's all just go to bed.'

'Have you double-checked?' asked Nicola.

Mrs Dugdale nodded, hard-done-by, world-weary.

From behind her back Nicola produced the purse, and offered it to Mrs Dugdale.

'Best check it one more time?'

'There's no point,' said Mrs Dugdale.

'I think there might be,' said her husband.

Nicola, still offering the purse, said: 'Once my mum thought someone had stolen her earrings, and she spent hours looking, and then she found them in her ears!'

Mrs Dugdale took the purse, impatiently, snapped it open, and began to count.

'There should be eighty, right? But in fact there's ten, twenty, thirty...' She counted down on to the arm of the armchair, in a distant, superior way, like a card sharper who knows what the hands are going to be, and is bored by his own skill. 'Fifty, sixty, seventy – ' She stopped.

She still had a ten pound note in her hand.

'Eighty,' said Nicola.

11

A Nice Little Walk

Emmy didn't sleep well, and the night went slowly. She woke for the umpteenth time at seven. Nicola was snoring on the lilo. Emmy felt restless, but she didn't get up. Getting up meant facing things, and things were in a mess.

Nothing had been sorted out last night. Obviously Nicola had stolen the money, and then put it back in the purse when she heard the row. Neither Mr nor Mrs Dugdale had said this outright. They'd probably been chewing it over, and over, after the girls had gone to bed, and this morning Nicola would get it in the neck.

Although in some ways Emmy relished this prospect, there was also a downside. Her parents wouldn't just give Nicola a big telling off. They'd want to know the ins and outs of the catflap. Why, when, how, where; deadly serious 'talks' and moralising and inquests; how there was a dividing line between horseplay, and theft; and if you let something happen it was as bad as doing it yourself.

Cringe!

It was easier to hide under the hot, smelly covers, and try and imagine what nasty home truths would be brought home to Nicola, and how she would react. Maybe she'd even start crying. That would be good. Very good indeed.

'Come on, sleepy head!'

Emmy's heart shot up into her throat. The voice was bright and full of energy. Mrs Dugdale was dressed, her hair done, her face made up. Although Emmy was wide awake, she pretended still to drowse, not daring to believe her mother's cheerful mood.

Mrs Dugdale had found Normous, and was preening the under-bed fluff from his fur.

'Come on, you two, we're going out. We've all been hanging around in this stuffy house for far too long. Haven't we, Normous?'

And she made Normous nod his small stupid head. To Nicola, she said nothing.

In the kitchen before Nicola came down, Mrs Dugdale, cooking breakfast, said casually to her daughter:

'About yesterday. That was all my fault, you understand? You mustn't feel bad about it. I'm very sorry for taking things out on you. I know what you've had to put up with. And I think in a way it's done me good, to get all my feelings out in the open like that. So, are we friends again?'

Emmy, although she couldn't be sure exactly which row or crisis Mrs Dugdale was referring to, ran to her, and hugged her. All the same, she kept an eye on the frying pan. Frying pans can be unpredictable, spitting at you when you least expect it.

'How about Dad?'

'He went to work ages ago.'

Just like him. The only day he gets up early is when he wants to avoid a difficult scene.

'Are you friends with him again too?'

'I hope so.'

Emmy would have liked to talk more, but Nicola sidled in, yawning. Emmy caught her breath. Now, surely, Nicola would get the Riot Act in spades.

Mrs Dugdale said nothing.

Emmy asked where they were going.

'Not the Puddleflumps again,' said Nicola.

'No,' replied Mrs Dugdale, 'they're not my cup of tea, I'm afraid.'

'How about Gloucester, have a look round the shops?'

'Plenty of time for that later in the week. When it's raining. Today, we're going to do something Healthy, outdoors. I've done a picnic.'

'Great,' Nicola said privately to Emmy, so Mrs Dugdale could hear, 'the middle of winter – just right for a picnic.'

Emmy ignored her. She decided they weren't speaking to each other, after all. Not till her mum gave Nicola the dressing-down she so richly deserved, anyway. She was on her mum's side.

'It'll be good,' she said, reassuringly. 'I'll take the small rucksack.'

'Look at that glorious sunshine,' said Mrs Dugdale, as they walked to the car. A watery sun was filtering through the grey clouds.

'There's loads of historical stuff in the Grossops area,' she went on, 'and if the worst comes to the worst there's plenty of nice walks.'

'Nothing like a nice walk,' said Nicola.

Emmy gave her a look.

'Whereabouts are the walks?'

Mrs Dugdale said she didn't know, but if they drove towards Tinderford they should find something.

'We might find some holly – or even some mistletoe.'

'Great', mouthed Nicola; but Mrs Dugdale took no notice.

So they set off, in the car, for a nice little walk, or something.

Mrs Dugdale drove around for a long time, looking for a National Trust Sign or a castle or anything, really. But they saw nothing, only pine forestation, rows upon rows of regular conifers, and every now and then a farm, or cottage, or housing estate.

'It's not like real countryside, is it?' asked Mrs Dugdale. Emmy said it was all right. Nicola said there were certainly plenty of Christmas trees.

'Anyway,' she added, 'my dad says there's no real countryside left any more.'

At one point, going down a lane that Mrs Dugdale thought might be promising, they came upon a row of buses and vans, tightly parked on the grass verge. The vehicles had been brightly painted in mauves and pinks, but the poor quality paint had quickly faded.

'Like Puddleflumps,' said Nicola.

The smells of paraffin and cooking and smoke were strong on the air.

Children stopped playing, and stared at the intruding car. Mrs Dugdale pulled up, not sure there was room to get past the parked vehicles, or whether she wanted to get past them.

A big shaggy dog loped over and sniffed at the door of the car. Mrs Dugdale edged away in her seat.

'That's like the one that came in our garden the day we moved in,' said Emmy.

Two or three other various, smaller dogs barked, and came over to join the big shaggy one.

'Always so many puppies,' observed Mrs Dugdale.

Nicola laughed: 'My dad says it's cos they eat them when they get full sized.'

'Let's go back,' Emmy urged.

Her stomach had started churning. Nicola leaned forward in her seat, coolly estimating the distance between the parked vehicles and the far hedge.

'There's plenty of room to get through, I'm sure,' she said.

Mrs Dugdale couldn't decide. She made strange jerky movements. For some reason she went to put her indicator on, but hit the wipers by mistake.

'What are you doing, Mum?'

Mrs Dugdale told Emmy to shut up.

Several adults had appeared round the camp fire, including the bald girl. She came up to the car, and signalled that Mrs Dugdale should wind down her window. Mrs Dugdale refused. Nicola wound down hers instead, and the conversation continued, between Mrs Dugdale and the girl, through Nicola, as through an interpreter.

The girl said there *was* enough room to get through, and she was sorry for the inconvenience. They were looking for a more suitable place to park; but it was certainly worth a drive up the lane because there was a small mountain, or hill at the end, which you could climb, where there was a sort of monument, and you could see for many miles.

Mrs Dugdale was not interested. She had made up her mind to go back. The trouble was, she couldn't find reverse gear. She kept looking over her shoulder, and thrusting at the gear stick, with much grinding and clashing: but every time she let out the clutch, the car sprang forwards, not back.

The bald girl said: 'If you want to turn round, there's a gateway about fifty yards past the camp. There's plenty of room there.'

After several more attempts to engage reverse, Mrs Dugdale took her advice. The bald girl guided her past the parked vehicles, although Mrs Dugdale pretended not to be taking any notice.

Once past the camp, Nicola said they might as well carry on to the hill, as they'd come this far. Mrs Dugdale ignored her. She didn't like having the travellers behind her, blocking her escape route. Emmy also ignored Nicola. She was glad they weren't staying here: she felt nervous in the narrow lane, too.

Mrs Dugdale managed to turn round in the gateway. Reverse gear was no trouble when there was no one watching. The rear wheels spun a bit in some mud, but she kept calm, and slowed the revs, and with a jump the car pulled clear. She also managed to drive past the camp without a guide on the way back. Emmy saw the big dog, and his big eyes, again, and felt silly, being scared of him. The bald girl waved, and the children shouted.

'Scum,' said Mrs Dugdale, and put her foot down, and drove back down the lane towards the main road much faster than she ought to have driven. Fortunately, she did not meet any traffic coming the other way.

After an hour, driving in circles, because she didn't want to stray too far from Slobowen, Mrs Dugdale parked the car. It wasn't a proper layby, just a sort of muddy patch near a fence where the road widened for a bit. Mrs Dugdale didn't park too accurately, either. She got the nearside wheels just over the lip of a low ditch, into some mud.

'Never mind,' she said.

Emmy could see her mum was in pain, again.

'Have you got your tablets?'

Mrs Dugdale replied that she had already taken two, just now.

'We better go back, if it's bad.'

Mrs Dugdale said, no, they wouldn't go back, because they'd come out for a nice walk and a nice walk they were going to have, and a picnic.

Nicola had explored the extent of the verge. She was not impressed.

83

'Where are we going?'

Mrs Dugdale pointed over the low wire fence, where a faint suggestion of a path ran away and disappeared into dense, wet undergrowth.

'What's that?'

'It's a walk,' replied Mrs Dugdale, getting her foot up onto the fence.

Emmy didn't like the look of the fence, or the path. It had private and snakes and big guard dogs written all over it:

'No, mum, come on, let's go home, it's horrible here, if you've got pains, I don't want to – '

Her mother pulled herself up onto the top of the fence, then jumped down on the other side.

'Mum!'

Nicola climbed easily up and over the fence, joining Mrs Dugdale. Emmy stayed by the car.

'Come on,' shouted Mrs Dugdale. 'It isn't high.'

'I don't want to.'

'Come on,' taunted Nicola. 'Even fat Shirley could get over that.'

It was then that Emmy remembered.

She was supposed to be going round to Shirley's today. Now. She had forgotten the arrangement completely, in the excitement of her mother's plans. Misery! What a great start to Be Fair to Shirley Week! Worse: now she *had* remembered, she didn't care. In fact, she was glad to be missing the visit.

'We'll push on ahead,' said Mrs Dugdale to Nicola. 'Madam'll soon catch us up.'

And Mrs Dugdale and Nicola strolled off together,

like they were the best of friends, leaving Emmy behind. The sight cut her to the heart. It was her mum, not Nicola's. Nicola was the guilty party, the thief, the one who kept making sarcastic comments. But there she was, there they were, going off together, leaving her behind, alone.

Not fair! Not fair at all.

And scary.

Emmy ran to the fence, pulled herself over it anyhow, snagging her jeans and anorak on the wire, and stumbled on towards the bushes into which Mrs Dugdale and Nicola had disappeared.

12

Not-talking

Emmy caught up with them after twenty or thirty metres. They were clambering through thick scrub. Mrs Dugdale, puffing a bit, turned a superior smile on her daughter:

'So you deigned to join us?'

Emmy said nothing. 'Us' should be her and her mother, not her mother and Nicola.

They emerged onto a wide path, that led upwards through the wood. Mrs Dugdale was triumphant. 'I bet it's just as good as that silly bald girl's walk.'

'It's probably the same one,' Nicola said.

Pushing through the bushes onto the path, Emmy made sure she was between her mother and Nicola. She took her mum's arm. Nicola shook her head pityingly, and drifted on ahead.

'Why haven't you told her off?' Emmy whispered.

'What for? Being cheerful?'

'You know what I mean, the ten pound note. It's obvious she took it.'

Mrs Dugdale frowned. 'There's no proof.'

'I saw her ... well, she was messing with it when we were washing up.'

'But you didn't actually see her take it?'

'No, but you could at least accuse her. I bet she'd cave in. If you put some pressure on.'

'I'm not the Gestapo. And she's a guest.'

'So she can do what she likes?'

'It's over now. The money's back. We've had enough bad feeling, haven't we?'

Emmy did not reply. She put her head down, and walked on ahead of her mother.

Quite soon she caught up with Nicola, who seemed to be waiting for her. She was making faces. Emmy looked away, to stop herself laughing. She wasn't going to be the one to speak first.

The path was broad now, wet, and thick with mud and ruts. Emmy would overtake Nicola, and press on alone, noble and brave and hard-done-by. Trouble was, although Emmy walked faster and faster, Nicola kept up easily. Emmy was nearly running, and Nicola seemed to be strolling, and was still making faces, inviting Emmy to laugh.

Emmy was beginning to feel pretty stupid, when a fat boy on a mountain bike passed them, going up the hill. He was pedalling hard, but the bike was moving very slowly.

Nicola shouted something to him about fighting the flab. Emmy's face went hot. The boy ignored them, standing up on his pedals and thrusting away with his fat legs, his back wheel skidding and hopping on the slippery leaves.

Nicola called again: 'Why don't you get off and roll?'

It wasn't very funny, but Emmy, despite herself, was grinning. This spurred Nicola on. She started chanting 'fat arse, fat arse'. Emmy struggled to keep her lips frozen serious, but little sobs of laughter puffed out. The boy turned his head, and stared at them for a moment, his mouth small on his big face, goggle-eyed, then he pedalled on, more furiously still, until he was out of sight.

Nicola was very pleased with herself.

'Come on, you want to laugh, why don't you? Did you fancy him? He was hunky, yeah?'

Emmy said she must be joking. Nicola pressed her:

'Come on, that's your kind of boy, admit it, the lean, sporty type.'

Emmy was angry with herself. What good was being off and not-talking to someone, if you started grinning and talking?

They had slowed to a dawdle, and Mrs Dugdale caught them up. She was gasping and although her cheeks were livid, there was a deep white beneath the red. As she came near, Emmy hunched her shoulders, and examined something in the undergrowth.

Mrs Dugdale asked what the boy had said to them.

Nicola, teasing the leaves from a wayside plant, left Emmy to answer the question:

'He didn't say anything.'

'Why were you shouting at him, then?'

'It was just a joke. ' She meant to sound casual,

but it came out irritable. Mrs Dugdale frowned:

'Honestly, Emmeline. I don't know what's got into you. You're just spoiling for a row, all the time, aren't you?'

And when Emmy said nothing:

'I think we better go home.'

'No!'

It came as a surprise to Emmy to realise she didn't want to turn back.

'If you can't go for a walk without... ' Mrs Dugdale didn't finish the sentence.

'It's got nothing to do with me,' Emmy shouted. 'What you mean, is, you're tired and you've had enough, so you want to find some excuse to go back, you don't want to take it on yourself, you want to put it on to me. That's what you mean. That's what you always do.'

Emmy turned her back.

'Course it doesn't matter, if you tell me,' said Mrs Dugdale, vaguely. Then to Nicola, in a rather silly, mumsy voice:

'Would you like to carry on, Nicky?'

Nicky shrugged. She would much rather be back in the warm, but she did not say so.

'Let's carry on a bit further, then. As long as you don't get too far away. It's easy to get lost out here. It's not like Page Park in Bristol.' Bristol was where Mrs Dugdale had grown up.

Neither of the girls had ever been to Page Park.

As they walked on, Nicola asked:

'Is your mum really ill?'

For a moment, Emmy considered not replying; but not-talking again seemed too childish.

'Course she is.'

'Is it something serious, like cancer?'

Emmy knew what the disease was, but couldn't pronounce the name.

'She's waiting to have an operation, but there's a waiting list, so it might be next year or even the year after.'

'But she's not going to die?'

'No.' Emmy remembered the phrase. 'It's not life-threatening.'

'Oh.' Nicola sounded disappointed. 'She's always moaning, isn't she?'

'Not always.'

'Well, pretty often.'

'She's in pain.'

'Yeah, but grown-ups, they should be used to it, shouldn't they? She's like a kid.'

Emmy said nothing. Dad said they were lucky she didn't have something life-threatening, but in a way that would be better, because she could tell people her mum was dying, and then they'd all say, oh dear, you poor thing. But just having this obscure disease, no one took it seriously, especially as the name was so hard to remember.

At which point, they came upon the river.

It was a real river, maybe three metres wide. The path crossed it by a stone bridge. Emmy ran on to the bridge, and peered over into the fast moving water. Nicola sauntered off left along the bank.

90

Emmy dropped her rucksack, threw two twigs over into the stream, and ran to the other side of the bridge. She couldn't be sure if she saw one or either of the twigs emerge. Nor could she have told them apart from each other, or from other bits and pieces caught in the stream. Pooh sticks has got to be the most overrated, boring game in the world. But, given a bridge and a river, it's hard not to do it, like scratching a bite.

When Emmy next looked, Nicola had disappeared. Emmy called, but there was no reply.

Emmy was alone, on the bridge.

She did not want to be alone. If she waited, her mum would come. Or Nicola would come back from up the river. So that was all right, wasn't it?

She waited, and her mother did not come. What if Mrs Dugdale had gone another way, or ceased to exist. What if Nicola had gone on, and wasn't coming back to the bridge, either? What if Nicola had taken offence, because Emmy hadn't replied to her last question. Maybe *she* was not-talking, now.

The waters ran, and the air sidled round the bare trees. It was like Emmy was the last person left in the world.

Like her first day at big school and everyone suddenly disappeared indoors and she was left standing in acres of tarmac, with all the sweet papers blowing, and it was deadly quiet, and she didn't have a clue where she should be, or why, and she'd gone into the nearest building, and knocked on a door that looked a bit like her form room, but it wasn't, it was full of big kids, and the teacher had made fun of her, and everyone had laughed.

Forcing herself to breathe slowly, and regularly, she walked back along the path to the edge of the woods.

No sign of her mum.

That did it. Emmy set off at full pelt along the river bank, after her friend.

13

Private

Round the bend, was another bend, and no sign of
Nicola. Emmy went on. She came upon a fence,
running from the bank of the river up into the woods,
and beyond. It was a wire fence, with a notice on it:

PRIVATE
NO FISHING
TRESPASSERS WILL BE PROSECUTED

Emmy's heart sank. Worse and worse. Better to
be at Shirley's house, under the eagle eye of Mrs
Bridle, shoes off in the hall and doilies. Where was
Nicola? Gone, gone private, trespassing. Mrs
Dugdale might have reached the bridge by now.
Best get back there.

'Come on, hurry up.'

Nicola, ahead, beyond the fence, waving.

'Come on, come and see what I've found.'

Nicola disappeared again, round the next bend.

Gingerly, Emmy picked her way over the fence.

What Nicola had found was a small wooden hut.

Whether or not it had been locked before Nicola found it, the door was now hanging loose to one side. Inside the hut was a boat.

'It's too heavy. I can't move it on my own,' Nicola explained. That's why she'd come back looking for Emmy.

'What are you going to do with it?'

Nicola said she was going to play the National Anthem on it.

'You get behind it and I'll pull on the rope.'

Emmy looked back up the river, hoping to see her mother. She saw nothing.

'I just want to see if it floats,' said Nicola.

'It said Private.'

'That's not the law, they can't stop you. My Dad says, there's no such thing as trespass. Anyway, it's really really old, I bet they've forgotten about it, whoever's it is.'

Emmy bit her lip. She had been taught different, all stuff about respecting other people's property and ending up in prison if you drop a sweet paper.

'Come on, you're such a wet willie.'

Emmy made up her mind. She crept into the shed. It was wormy-smelling, fishy. Probably lots of big spiders. Emmy tried not to think about the spiders, clambering round behind the boat. The boat was resting on a slipway of small logs, which led down to the water's edge. Emmy started pushing. The boat moved easily. Either she was much stronger than Nicola, or Nicola hadn't been trying very hard. The other girl had to jump out of the way, as the boat slithered and creaked down over the logs, and splashed into the water.

At once, Emmy set off back along the river bank, towards the bridge and the path. Nicola, painter in hand, shouted after her:

'Where are you going?'

'I left my rucksack.'

Mum must be there by now.

'Coward. Yellow belly. Wally.'

Emmy, hot inside, climbed over the fence, and ran as fast as she could back to the bridge.

There was no one there.

She couldn't tell whether her mother had not yet arrived, or had been and gone. The rucksack sagged where she had dropped it. Panic welled up inside her. She forced herself to be calm, to wait, to listen.

There were no sounds, but the water running, and something, droning, and every now and then a distant crash: bird scarer? Gun? She couldn't even hear Nicola, although she was only a hundred yards away, and was probably making as much noise as possible.

She found a pen in her rucksack, and a sheet of pink paper, and wrote on it:

'MUM, go left, past fence, boat hut, Em'. She put the note on top of the rucksack, and weighed it down with a big stone.

She walked along the bank towards the fence, looking back over her shoulder every few paces. It occurred to her that a thief might come along and take the rucksack, and the note, and she wanted to go back. But she could now hear Nicola, singing, and she carried on.

What if her mother had overtaken them, and was pressing on along the path on the other side of the river? Shouldn't they follow, now, and catch her up? But then, what if she was still behind? Climbing the fence, Emmy swallowed the panic feelings as well as she could. If the worst came to the worst, they would just have to follow the path back to the car, and wait for Mrs Dugdale there. Mum would have to go back there eventually, wouldn't she?

Yes! Course she would. Everything would turn out OK. Then there was the picnic. She was beginning to feel hungry.

Suddenly free from all grudges and guilts, convinced that everything would work out for the best, Emmy charged off towards the bend in the river.

Nicola had not yet managed to get herself into the boat. She tiptoed at the water's edge, balancing on the timber runners, pulling at the rope, stretching out one foot, then the other, but never having the nerve to make the final step. Emmy felt a surge of scorn, and superiority: two years ago, she had gone on a boating weekend with the Guides.

'Just hold the side, like this, to keep it steady.'

Nicola did as she was told.

'Hang on.'

Emmy went back into the hut. She felt about the walls, and as her eyes became accustomed to the gloom, found two oars. Maybe her mum had come over bad before she got anywhere near the bridge, and was now lying on the path, helpless. Maybe she'd heard them talking, and was now going to prove it *was* life-threatening, whatever she had. That'd show Nicola.

Emmy shivered.

She emerged from the hut briskly. She stowed the oars in the boat, which Nicola was still holding, obedient. Emmy rather liked this unusual superiority over her friend. Seeming more calm and confident than she actually was, she took a single big step right into the middle of the boat. It rocked a bit, but she held onto the freeboard on each side, and sat down on the centre seat, facing backwards.

'How about me?' Nicola asked.

'Hang on.'

Emmy used one of the oars to lever the boat hard into the slipway, and held it there, wedged.

'Get in now, it won't move.'

Nicola stepped into the boat. She was timid, and stiff, so she only put her foot just over the freeboard, and the boat dipped, and might have turned over, if Emmy had not had it propped so firmly. Nicola sat herself down on the thwarts at the back of the boat, facing Emmy, and crossed her arms with exaggerated pomp, like an emperor.

'Right, slave,' she said. 'Row!'

14

Tramps' Landing

Emmy pushed the boat off the mud, and turned it towards the bridge. They had to go back to the bridge, so why not go in the boat? And if this let her show off how well she could row ... why not? And if her mum *was* there ... well, she probably wouldn't be, not till after they'd put the boat back.

'You're facing the wrong way, aren't you?' Nicola said.

'That's the way you sit, rowing,' explained Emmy. 'You're the cox.'

Nicola giggled.

'It means you've got to tell me where to go.'

And that's what Nicola did.

The first bend, she steered Emmy on purpose into the mud under a wild willow, but Emmy got so cross, Nicola did it properly after that. And it was good, once they got going, working as a team. Emmy rowed easily, but fast, adjusting to the right or left as Nicola indicated.

It was like that trust game in drama, where you have to fall backwards, and trust that the other person will catch you. It was a good feeling, a very good feeling, being a team, with Nickie, trusting.

They shot under the bridge.

Emmy stopped rowing, steered for the bank. There was no one on the bridge, no sign of anyone near the bridge, no sign of anyone anywhere.

'Don't stop! We're really flying!'

'I know, but I left a note for Mum.'

Nicola had forgotten about Mrs Dugdale. 'Oh, her,' she said.

'I won't be two seconds.'

Emmy ran the boat firmly onto the mud where the bank dipped down to the water, and scrambled out. Nicola sat where she was, looking about her, twisting her hair in her fingers. She looked like a queen, a beautiful pampered queen, and Emmy was her servant.

Emmy hurried to the rucksack, hoping Nicola wouldn't get bored with boating before she got back.

The note was still on the rucksack, the rucksack was still on the bridge. Quickly, quickly. What to do? She remembered that it wasn't their boat. Nicola called out: 'Come on, slave, for goodness sake.'

They were borrowing – no, hiring it. They'd pay, wouldn't they? – if anyone asked, like you do at Ladram Bay.

Nicola was yawning, and stretching. She might get out of the boat any minute, and the whole thing would be spoilt.

'Just coming,' Emmy shouted.

She looked at her watch. 1.35. She tore off a new piece of notepaper, with a cute cartoon cat in pink on the corner, and wrote:

'MUM, Gone exploring, won't go far, back at 2.30. Love Emmy. PS, hope you're OK.' She put the note on the parapet of the bridge, weighed down with the big stone. She took the rucksack, with the picnic and drink in it.

Nicola, in the boat, was stretching and rubbing her back.

'Right,' said Emmy, very businesslike, climbing aboard, 'we've got an hour. We come back here at 2.30.'

'What, an hour?' Nicola whined, like 7Q1 when the supply teacher says it's maths. In the five minutes they had been stopped, she had managed to conquer her enthusiasm for coxing.

'Come on,' urged Emmy, 'it was good, really good.'

'Oh, yes, *great*.'

Emmy pushed the boat away from the bank.

'Come on, steer.'

Nicola yawned. 'Do I have to?'

'Yes. You were enjoying it, it was fun.'

'Oh, well.'

And Nicola steered again, but in a bored, off-hand way, like a parent reading one story too many at bedtime. The boat glided smoothly along on the water. Emmy thought, once they got going, Nickie would get drawn into the spirit again, that they'd

100

start flying, working as a team; but she was disappointed. Nickie, playing bored, began to mess about.

Emmy's palms were tingling, and she'd probably end up with blisters, and they'd stolen the boat, and lost her mother. But it was better than spending a day at Shirley's.

She started. A vibration, gathering volume, like slow thunder, getting nearer, suddenly over them, deafening.

'It's just an aeroplane, you wally,' Nicola said.

Emmy had frozen. She tried to row again, casually. The sound died away, in eddies of echoes, far away on the mountains of Wales.

It was gloomy on the river, the trees looming high, often meeting overhead to mask the sky. The sun was on its way down, behind thick grey clouds. The air shone a dull yellow, the bushes stuck out unreal, like through 3D glasses.

Nicola was getting very noisy, and doing less and less serious steering. She sang songs, shouted rude things at imaginary people on the river bank, told jokes, and imitated telly ads. At first Emmy was scared of someone hearing, then, she began to hope that they *would* see someone, anyone.

'Time to turn back, then,' Emmy said, and began to manoeuvre the boat round.

'Why, what time is it?'

Emmy looked at her watch. 'Ten to.'

'That's not half way,' exclaimed Nicola scornfully. 'We've hardly started. If we've got an hour, that's half an hour out, and half an hour back.'

101

Emmy said they only had fifty five minutes.

'So,' said Nicola, 'we turn round at two and one half minutes past two.'

Emmy now plied the oars with less energy. All the excitement had gone out of the adventure. She just wanted to get it over with. Then it would be fun, afterwards, talking about it, telling people.

Nicola, on the other hand, had found new enthusiasm.

'Come on slave, you're slacking!'

'It's hard work.'

'Don't worry, I'll row back. Now, faster, faster, faster.'

At five past two, Emmy made to turn round, but Nicola wouldn't let her.

'We've got to find a proper landing place.'

Facing the wrong way, Emmy saw spot after spot slipping behind them which would have been perfectly OK for landing and swapping round. It was nearly quarter past two when at last she took things into her own hands, and pulled into a broad pool. The water there was standing, aside from the current, and the banks were steep. Emmy shivered, from cold, and from bad feelings.

She wanted to go to the lavatory, urgently.

It wasn't easy to scramble up and on to the bank. She got mud slicks on her jeans and anorak. She ran into the bushes, and pulled down her jeans.

As she squatted, Emmy took in the spot. Most of the ground was covered with reeds, yellow, hard, two or three feet high.

'Nickie?'

No answer.

She pulled up her jeans, and walked back to the boat. If she panicked, if she rushed, the nutters and perverts who lived here, and who were now hiding among the long hard reeds, would jump out and capture her and take her prisoner and keep her here for ransom.

The boat was empty.

As Emmy looked quickly about her, something wet and squidgy hit her cheek.

'Got you!' Nickie, who had been crouching among the reeds, stood up. Emmy wiped her face. She didn't investigate the missile.

'Come on, let's go. It's horrible here.'

'No, we've got to explore, haven't we? What's the point of coming if we don't explore?'

Nickie waded away through the reeds, and Emmy, reluctantly, followed. Although she'd only just been, she felt she wanted the toilet again.

'Look at that!'

Nickie had broken through into a flat area where the reeds had been stamped down. In the middle of this there was a scorched patch, with stones and a few rusted tins.

'It's so spooky it's wicked,' she said, picking up a tin. 'Corned beef. That means tramps. Only tramps eat corned beef. They put the tin in the fire and when it explodes they know it's done.'

'Come on, let's go.' Emmy was shivering all the time now, big shivers that came from the pit of her stomach, and which made her slack mouth stammer as she spoke.

'My dad says they don't pay any poll tax, it's disgusting. Look, here's a pair of pants.'

Nicola held up on the end of a stick a damp scrap of cloth, that might have been underwear, or a scarf, or a rag, or anything.

'OK, OK, let's go.'

Nickie threatened Emmy with the rag. Emmy squealed, and flinched away.

'I wonder what they get up to here at night?' mused Nicola, flicking the damp cloth far into the bushes.

'I expect they sleep and try and keep warm. Come on!'

They made their way back to the boat. Emmy scrambled onto the rear thwart. Nicola wasn't finished, yet. She raised her stick like a queen with a sword:

'I name this place, Tramps' Landing.'

'Come on, I'm freezing to death here.'

Still Nicola remained above her on the bank.

'We ought to leave some trap or something, so when they come back – ' Nicola tried to think of something to finish the plan: 'Like a pit they fall into or something, with spikes in it, or a tree that shoots up and catches their ankle.'

Emmy was frantic. 'If you don't get back in *now*, I'm going without you.'

She lifted an oar, to show she meant business. Nicola stood above her, hands on her hips, shaking her head.

'You are a case, aren't you? You really do take after your fudging mother.'

'Come on,' said Emmy, yet again. Being reminded of her mother did not add to her peace of mind.

'You see,' Nicola went on, 'you just haven't got the guts to do anything on your own, let alone leave me here. I could stand up here for an hour and you wouldn't dare go without me. You're scared witless.'

'Please.' Emmy was near tears. The air seemed uglier than ever, yellow going grey. She looked at her watch. It was gone half two.

They were late.

Nicola made Emmy wait another thirty seconds, to prove her point, before she slid down into the boat, and took the oars.

Nickie was not an oarsperson. She had not been on a Girl Guides Boat Afloat weekend. She didn't know how to hold the oars, she didn't know which way to move them, she pushed and pulled and pulled and pushed, and the boat slid round in half circles, and drifted on down the river away from Tramps' Landing, further away from the bridge.

In an ecstasy of panic and irritation, Emmy tried to show her how to do it properly. At last, Nicola got into some semblance of a rhythm with both her oars cooperating: but she insisted on doing it 'pusher' style, each stroke starting under her chin, and ending with the extension of her arms.

'That's so weedy,' complained Emmy.

'Yes, but at least I can see where I'm going.'

'Doing it like that, you won't be going anywhere.'

105

And Emmy was right. While Nicola messed about, they had slipped thirty or forty metres down from Tramps' Landing, further away from the bridge, and now she was barely holding her own against the current. Still, she seemed to find it all most amusing, the splashes of water that shot off the blades and into the boat, the way the boat twisted and squirmed about under the uneven pressure of her rowing.

Finally, Emmy could bear it no longer, and begged Nicola to let her row. For a bit, Nicola refused, and rowed even worse on purpose, and made silly jokes; but she wasn't enjoying herself, and soon handed the oars back to Emmy.

When they had changed places, Emmy found their lack of progress wasn't entirely due to Nicola's stupidity and incompetence. There was a strong current, taking them away from the bridge.

It was ten to three.

Emmy tried to pull steadily. Her palms were stinging. Blisters had come up, and were now burst by the pressure of the oars. Gradually, she made some progress, and they came abreast of Tramps' Landing. Her watch said five past three. Time seemed to be gushing away like water from a burst pipe.

In looking at her watch, she had missed several strokes, and the current carried the boat several yards below Tramps' Landing again. Very tired, Emmy pulled hard, and managed to get the boat out of the current into the standing water. There, she rested. Her chest was tight, and sore, her breathing came in painful sobs.

'O slave, why stoppest thou?' cried Nicola in a silly voice.

'Shut your mouth, Nic,' snapped Emmy.

15

Wet

Emmy fought with herself, to keep cool. She must think about the situation they were in, and how to get out of it.

From the bridge, it had taken thirty-five, forty minutes of strong rowing to get to Tramps' Landing. Against the stream rowing equally strongly must take at least an hour and a half, but she couldn't row strongly, not even for half an hour. Her hands were badly blistered, her chest ached, the muscles of her neck were in spasm.

The sums wouldn't add up.

It was like one of her regular nightmares, when she has to get to school, but every movement is like wading through treacle, and more and more things get in the way – locks to be unlocked for which keys must be found, dirty men hiding keys beyond high fences, and train journeys that would take ten hours if the train wasn't broken down.

Nicola's cold voice cut in on her thoughts: 'I spect they've started eating her by now.'

She was lounging, idly scooping at the water with her hand, like a princess after a parade, bored, waiting for her servants to take her off to her palace.

'What do you mean?'

'Your mum. I expect she collapsed in the forest, crying out for help all feeble like she does, and then she died, and all the little toothy animals are scuttling about waiting for it to get dark so they can come and eat her.'

Emmy stood up, and tried to pull herself out of the boat on to the bank. Probably because she was rattled, her mind hurried and blurred with fear, she had not fastened the boat securely this time, and it slid away from under her. Hanging on to the bank, pressing with her knees against the side of the boat, she managed to preserve a risky equilibrium.

'Nic, get hold of that tree.'

Nicola did not do as she was told.

'I thought you could handle a boat,' she said.

The boat was slipping backwards, Emmy's sore hands losing their grip on the hard reeds and loose grasses of the bank.

'Please, Nickie!'

'Oh, shut up!'

And Nicola leaned down, picked up the free oar, and thrust it hard into the bank. The boat slithered, Emmy's grasp on the reeds was wrenched free, for a moment she tottered, her knees poised on the free-board, her hands scrabbling at the mud and plants down the bank: then she splashed, gulping, into the river.

For a moment, she could not believe that her warm body was actually in the dark, cold water. She was irritated, as though it was a silly mistake, and any moment some big hand would reach down and lift her out, and apologise.

No hand came to help her.

She was choking. Her anorak was swollen up stupid with air and water, her trainers fat and heavy on her feet.

She struggled to the surface, and gasped in – not air, but more water, because it wasn't the surface, the surface was miles above her, and she had no air left, and her eyes were stinging and her lungs, and her hands, and her jeans were shrinking round her legs, strangling them.

She felt like staying there, just to show how hard done by she was, and then they'd all be sorry, but more water caught in her throat, and her nose exploded at the back with biting pain, and she thrust up further, and did break the surface, coughing and spluttering.

Nicola was laughing. It was the worst kind of forced schoolyard laugh, without warmth: the laughter of bullies at the misfortunes of their victims.

Emmy tried to get out some words about how stupid and how dangerous, but the words tripped and caught each other in the narrow gate of her throat. She had enough to do to keep her head above the water.

'Serves you right,' said Nicola. 'Scaredy. Telling people to shut up all the time. Anyway, it's only a bit of water.'

She had the rucksack on her lap. She was opening a can of orange.

Emmy swam over to a tree whose roots were exposed, and managed to pull herself up onto the bank. Her head was full of things she wanted to say to Nicola, but the words would not form up into sentences. Jostling them all out of the way was outrage, about the orange. That was her can, Nic's was Coke. It wasn't fair.

Emmy took off her anorak, and tried to wring the water out of it. Every time she moved, her trainers squelched. Her nose ached at the back. Nicola was guzzling the orange.

'That's my drink,' Emmy said. 'I chose that.'

She knew it was stupid, as soon as she said it.

The keen air busied itself among her wet clothes. She shivered. The light was fading fast. Gone three. Half past? She looked at her watch, but could make no sense of it.

It was urgent for her to get moving. The wet clothes were slimy and cold on her skin, heavy and stinking with stagnant water. She was shivering in big shudders right from the centre of her body. It would remain light for half an hour, forty minutes – or less? Wasn't it the shortest day? The calculation made her giddy with fear. She must get back to the bridge, and from there to the car.

But, she could not leave Nicola.

She could not leave her, not because she cared about her friend, but because she feared to be alone.

She moved to the bank, and squatted above the boat.

Nicola tossed the empty orange can far into the river. The current caught it, and plucked it away and out of sight.

'Come on, then,' she said, 'let's go.'

Emmy's jaw trembled as she replied. She said, in a thin, impersonal voice, that it was impossible to row against the stream back to the bridge.

'Oh, don't talk crap,' Nicola snapped. 'Just get in and row. I'm cold.'

And she laughed.

'Just because you got a bit wet and I made a joke about your mother.'

'We'll have to make our way back to the bridge along the bank, on foot.'

'Speak for yourself.'

'Nicola, I'm serious. I'm not joking. I'm going now. If you want to stay here all night, that's up to you.'

Emmy rose, and turned. Please, come with me. Please.

'Hang about, then, Em.'

Nicola was levering herself up off the seat.

'Here.' She tossed the rucksack up onto the bank, and held out her arm, and waited to be helped out of the boat.

16

Relaxing

Mr Dugdale vaulted out of the Landrover, pleased with himself. He hadn't actually sold any fertilizer, but he had got chatting with a farmer over Llandowtid way who needed some repairs to his milking shed, and Mr Dugdale had given a quote, and he felt there was a good chance he would get his first ever professional carpentry job.

So, he'd decided to take the afternoon off. He wanted to share this good news with his family (who would by now have got over any awkward moments about the purse). Although he felt quite blameless in the whole matter, he'd stopped in Llandowtid to buy flowers for his wife. Then he thought he ought to get something for Emmy, but there wasn't much, until fortunately, in the newsagents, he found the Puddleflump Annual.

Carrying it proudly, he marched into the house, ready to be welcomed, and praised. All rows would be forgotten. They'd all be happy, and warm, and, in his case, slightly drunk, like in Dickens.

The note on the kitchen table told him that his wife had taken the girls out for the day. Mr Dugdale felt left-out, and hard-done-by. His wife was obviously trying to outdo him in the Good Parenting stakes. The house, deserted, was cold and quiet.

Mr Dugdale decided to relax. He opened a can of beer, and put the TV on, and watched some rugby. He didn't like rugby, but it was comforting, seeing all those fat men get bruised and muddy while you were warm indoors. In fact, it started to get quite exciting, towards the end.

He finished the can, and threw it towards the bin. The can teetered and then fell to the floor. The bin was full. For a minute he tried to ignore the bin and the can, and concentrate on the struggles of the rugby players to score vital points: but it was too irritating.

He snatched up the can and the bin, and hurried to the kitchen. While he was at it, he would empty all the other bins. That would make one good black bin liner-full. Ten minutes still to go in the match. Plenty of time.

Galloping upstairs, he collected the bin from his own room, and the frog basket from Emmy's. Back in the kitchen he shook the frog basket over the bin liner. Nothing came out but a few tissues and sharpenings.

Six minutes to go. Next door, the commentator was getting excited.

The frog basket was always awkward to empty. Things got stuck, and then you had to put your hand in the frog's mouth, to make him regurgitate. And that could be unpleasant, because, despite hundreds

114

of warnings, Emmy was still inclined to put wet, or soggy, or vegetable things in the frog, which stuck to his wicker insides, and rotted.

Gingerly, Mr Dugdale reached into the frog's mouth. His hand came upon a paper bag. That was the problem. He pulled it out.

17

Alone

There was no path. The bank was thick with reeds and grasses. Trees stuck out their branches at odd angles, awkward heights.

Emmy led, and tried to set a good pace. Nicola dawdled along behind. She still seemed to think that this was all unnecessary, and that in the end Emmy would row her back to the bridge in style.

After they had walked for about five minutes, Nicola said: 'I'm starving. Let's have something to eat.'

Emmy realised that she too was hungry – ravenous. But she insisted they keep going. 'Come on. We'll have something at the bridge.'

As Emmy had the rucksack, there wasn't much Nicola could do, except drag her feet, and complain all the time about being stung and pricked and the damage it was doing to her trainers. She stopped to examine her arm, where a thorn had caught her. And, although impatient to get on, Emmy waited, while the light faded.

It was hard to know how much progress they were

making. The ground was always difficult. It was tempting to take easier paths away from the river, but if they lost the river, then they wouldn't have a clue where they were, and the thought of wandering in the woods in the dark filled Emmy with dread. Her clothes were now lukewarm on her skin, clinging, restricting. If she made an unusual movement, some new cranny of her body would meet wet cloth, cold and shocking.

Again Nicola stopped. 'Why can't we go straight back to the car?'

'Because we don't know the way straight back to the car.'

'Yeah, but if the bridge is this way, then the car must be that way. I'm sure it is, over there.'

Emmy peered in the direction Nicola was pointing. There were no lights, no sounds. Through the trees, very close, loomed the low ash-purple mountains, which she knew were twenty miles away.

Emmy needed the toilet again. She dropped the rucksack, forced her way a couple of paces into the bushes, and pulled down her jeans.

Nicola called: 'There's a path here. I bet it goes to the road.'

'Let's just keep going to the bridge,' pleaded Emmy. 'It can't be far, now.'

'I'm going this way. It must lead somewhere.'

Emmy, crouching in the bushes, couldn't see her friend. Nor could she make water. She was too tense.

'We've got to stay by the river, that's what it says in the book. It's so easy to get lost.'

'The book,' snorted Nicola. 'That's your whole life, books. You never actually do anything. You just read about it. You're such a coward, a goodie-goodie, you never do anything in case anyone catches you and tells you off. There's no one here to tell you off.'

'It's not that,' pleaded Emmy. 'This is dangerous, round here.'

'Oh, yeah. It isn't the jungle, you know, it isn't Everest. It's England and it's nearly Christmas.'

'It's not England, it's Wales, and this is a Danger Zone.'

This wasn't strictly true. Looking at a map of Wales, she had seen the words 'Danger Zone' in red capitals, and asked her father what it meant. He said it referred to the mountains off to the North West, where there were very few people, and houses, and the weather was often bad.

'So we're not in the Danger Zone here?'

'No, but we're very close, only about twenty miles away.'

That was quite close enough, for her imagination. She often got the map out, and looked at the words, 'Danger Zone', and tried to imagine what it would be like to be in Danger, in that Zone, and what those dangers were. At least now, the thought of Danger relaxed her muscles, and her water splashed down onto the ground.

Emmy pulled up her jeans.

'Nickie?'

No reply. The only sound was the rushing of the river behind her.

Nicola had gone.

Emmy moved a couple of paces after her friend. Vaguely, she expected to trip against something on the path, but didn't. For a moment she puzzled with herself why the path shouldn't be clear. Then she realised.

Nicola had taken the rucksack.

Fear overwhelmed Emmy, prickling on her scalp, rumbling in her stomach. Her skin glowed fever hot under the damp clothes.

'Wait for me!'

She plunged along the trail. She knew it was stupid. She knew the path would lead nowhere but into the heart of the woods, deep dark secret places without lights, where animals guarded their lairs, and tramps left rusty cans and soggy wads of old lavatory paper. But she couldn't bear to be alone.

The path got narrower, disappeared up against a bush. She stopped, and listened. Nothing. She called, her voice hardly above a whisper. Silly! She screamed out, and listened, and there was no sound, not the river, nor rustling: no sound but the silence, pressing on her eardrums. 'Nickie, don't play games, I'm scared. Please. Where are you?'

The sky was a fading grey above the splintery trees. The bushes around her spread and grew in shadow. She shouted again, and listened. Her heart fluttered, and she was breathing fast. She forced herself to breathe slower, deeper, to think.

She thought: even if the car is near here, the bridge can't be far away, either. The path from the bridge is really wide, even in the dark I'll be able to follow it, and even if the car's not there when I get to the road, there was a garage not very far away, or a pub or restaurant or something – her brain refused to deal with these details. The big thing was: if she got to the bridge, she would be all right – so long as she wasn't eaten by monsters on the way through the under-growth. But that was a silly, childish idea. There's no such thing as monsters, are there? Not when you're twelve.

Her stomach rumbled. She called, once more: 'Nicola, I'm going back along the river. If you want to come, come now. If not, whoever gets back, tell them where the other one is.' That didn't make much sense, but it was the best she could do. Hearing her own voice, her heart had started pounding again. She straightened her shoulders, and turned.

She turned carefully, trying to measure 90, then 180 degrees. This was a trick she'd read in a very old Girl Guide book, which her dad had bought her for a joke, published in the 30s, all about survival. Then, as though picking her way in the dark through an unfamiliar room among treasured procelain, she headed, she hoped, for the river.

It had taken only seconds for her to cover the distance away from the river. Now, minutes passed, and she could not find her way back. She heard the water, but could not get near to it. She fought a panic desire to run, anywhere.

Listening carefully, she was sure the water was off to her left. And, after another couple of minutes, she found it. Then it was clear what the difficulty had been. At the point that she had left the river, it bent away to the right. Emmy had been wandering in the blank area where the river would have been if it had gone straight on.

She looked at her watch. She forced herself to read its face. Three fifty. Another twenty minutes, and she'd made no further progress. Struggling through treacle. For several seconds, more, nearly a minute, she stood by the river, staring down towards the water. She kept telling herself to move, but it was so quiet, so calm, it was as if any movement would upset the gods of the place, and they would be cross with her. It was easier just to stand there, her eyes staring blankly into the invisible water.

Then, a big shiver erupted from the pit of her stomach, and she turned, and set off along the bank again.

18

Why Worry?

After the business with the boy on his mountain bike, Mrs Dugdale relaxed. She didn't have the energy to keep on and on at Emmy. Her daughter was twelve, now. She must be allowed to make her own mistakes. Loosen up! There was nothing she could do.

That was a pleasant, free feeling, strolling along the damp forest path, the edge of the pain in her stomach now blurred by the pain-killers, knowing the girls were somewhere ahead of her, but not exactly knowing where, and feeling no immediate responsibility for them. They could do as they pleased. And why not? What harm could possibly come to them, here?

On the bridge, she saw the sagging rucksack, heard the girls' voices. She lingered, leaning on the parapet, watching scum sucking beneath her among the reeds, expecting Emmy to appear, and run up, and hug her, or tell her some little bit of news about what she'd been up to.

She waited a minute, two minutes.

Why? It was tedious, hanging around waiting for your life to be lived for you by your daughter. She ought to be living her own life.

Mrs Dugdale walked on, over the bridge and on into the trees on the other side. She had not gone far along the path when she heard running steps. Turning, she saw Emmy arrive on the bridge, breathless.

Her daughter, anxious, looked this way and that, but did not see Mrs Dugdale. Mrs Dugdale was going to step out of the cover of the trees, and greet Emmy.

She did not.

It was interesting to watch her daughter, scurrying about, having to think for herself. Mrs Dugdale smiled as Emmy opened her rucksack, produced pencil and paper, and wrote a note. Sensible girl.

Mrs Dugdale intended to reveal herself at the last moment: but when the last moment came, and Emmy scampered off, Mrs Dugdale stayed where she was, hidden. She stood for a minute or two, looking back at the bridge. It was tempting to go back and read the note, but Mrs Dugdale couldn't be bothered. She'd done enough interfering.

She turned, and strolled on along the path.

She walked for ten, fifteen, twenty minutes, every minute thinking of halting, or returning, to see how the girls were doing: but every minute she resisted. It was delicious, to be selfish for once.

It was pleasant to stroll on, her head light, her stomach hot with stifled pain, stretching and stretching the bonds that bound her to Emmy, like a game, seeing how far she could go, never quite believing that the bonds might snap. It was a dangerous game, and exciting, and it would turn out OK. Things always did. That's what Peter said. Things turn out how they turn out whether you worry or not: so why worry?

She worried.

Each step now was a crime against her love for her daughter, but she took that step, and more steps, the guilt building up in her heart hot and thrilling.

Isn't it also a crime to stifle the growing child with too much anxiety, to protect too much?

Watching the toddler stretch his hand up towards the handle of a boiling saucepan, how long do you go on waiting before you intervene? Or do you wait for the crash, and the pain, and then say: 'I told you so?'

Disgusted with herself, she turned, and walked back briskly, expecting soon to hear the girls' voices, to see them strolling along towards her, heads together, discussing boys or pop or whatever they talked about.

No sign of the girls. No sound but rustling. A jet plane glided silently overhead, pursued by the angry blast of its engines.

She reached the bridge. The rucksack was no longer there. Mrs Dugdale called. She peered up and down stream. She found the note.

'MUM, Gone exploring, won't go far, back at 2.30. Love Emmy. PS, hope you're OK.'

She breathed easier. It was now just after two. She leaned on the parapet of the bridge. Exploring! But the PS was touching. And they were safe, of course. And she had twenty five minutes to wait.

More waiting!

She thought of all that Emmy had had to put up with over the last year or so, and she told herself off. What was twenty-five minutes to wait? For your only child? What joy would she feel, seeing Emmy return, reliable and on time, at 2.30, or more probably, just after?

So, Mrs Dugdale wrapped her coat closer round her, and thrust her hands into the pockets, and made up her mind to wait cheerfully, and not be irritable with her daughter when she turned up. Then they could all three have their picnic together, like a proper day out.

Emmy did not turn up at 2.30, or just after. Mrs Dugdale struggled to keep her good humour.

She ate her crispbreads and her apple, but saved the yoghurt, so she had something to eat along with the girls. Any moment she expected to see Emmy, running and laughing, or maybe loitering and moaning, if she'd had a row with Nicola. In her head, she carefully shaped the first thing she'd say: 'What time do you call this?' pointing at her watch, but humorous. Above all, she must be humorous.

Until three, Mrs Dugdale forced herself not to worry. At ten past three, she began to panic.

She read the note over again, as best she could, although the words jumped over each other and would not settle into a coherent order. It seemed to her quite possible that the girls meant to meet her

125

back at the car, not here at the bridge. A shiver ran through her. How stupid she was! How stupid her daughter was, and the note. She tried to keep calm, and read it again, but now the words whirled round like snowflakes in a blizzard. The light was failing.

She set off back towards the car. She stopped. She ought to leave a note, herself. She had neither pencil, nor pen. She ran back to the bridge. With her eyebrow pencil, she wrote on the parapet, in big shaky letters:

GONE TO CAR, MUM. THAT WAY

– with an arrow.

Then, she ran.

The car was still there on the verge, dewing up with big blobs of moisture. There was no sign of any girls or daughters. Mrs Dugdale listened. Maybe, somewhere, miles away, a tractor chugging. It had only taken her twelve minutes to get here from the bridge. Her shoes were ruined. She was out of breath. Her anxiety was beginning to include anger: why did Emmy have to keep doing things like this?

She tried to ignore the moisture on the car, which probably meant it wouldn't start. She opened the door, found the pen which Mr Dugdale made sure was always there (in case of accidents, for the taking down of particulars), and wrote another note.

GONE BACK TO BRIDGE WHERE ARE YOU
I'M SICK AND TIRED –

She screwed that note up, and wrote another.

GONE BACK TO BRIDGE, 3.35. WAIT HERE.
DOOR OPEN.

She switched the wipers on. It took a couple of goes to get them upright. Behind one of them she put the note. She turned back to the fence, put one foot on it, then returned to the car. She opened the boot, and found the yellow wellies that Mr Dugdale made sure were always there for emergencies. Balancing awkwardly on the muddy grass, she put the boots on.

Then she took the note off the windscreen, and screwed it up. It was stupid, telling any Tom or Dick who happened to come past that the car was unlocked. The new note read:

GONE BACK TO BRIDGE, 3.41. WAIT HERE.

She locked the car. It was more important that the car should be there, than that it should be open. After all, she would be back in half an hour.

In fact, it took her over twenty minutes to get to the bridge, by which time it was nearly pitch dark. Why hadn't she thought to bring the big flashlight, which Mr Dugdale also made sure was always in the boot, for emergencies?

She waited at the bridge for a few minutes, called out a few times (but not very loudly), then set off back to the car. She couldn't keep still. As soon as she stopped moving, she started to worry. Anxiety and guilt pumped up through her blood, until her head was light and giddy. The only antidote was anger, anger that her daughter should have put her through all this.

It was after half past four when she got back to the car. In the dark, the path was not easy to follow, even though she'd been along it so often.

She found the flashlight. It worked. She climbed back over the fence, and set off up the path. She came back, and switched on the car lights, set off up the path again, stopped, ran back to the car, switched off the lights. Mr Dugdale was always going on about the battery and how quickly it ran down with the lights on and the engine off, and she could hardly leave the engine running, could she?

She was halfway over the fence, the flashlight beam flying crazily up and over the trees, when a small voice called out from her right:

'Mrs Dugdale, is that you?'

19

Not a Life Preserver

The darkness loomed into Emmy's eyes, and billowed out into the spaces of her head. She collided with things that weren't there, and held out her hands to grasp imaginary fences and bushes. She was wet, and tired, and the ground was soft under her feet.

It would be good to lie down, and rest.

Not yet, not just yet. To rest she must find somewhere clear for the length of her body, no reeds –

She crashed into the sapling.

Her nose and the sinuses round her eyes flared and pulsed with pain. Tears of frustration, of self-pity welled up. Another mistake, and all her own fault. A silly thing to do.

Or, maybe God had put the sapling there so she would know she ought to rest? She sat down, and leaned against the tree.

The darkness turned white in her head and rushed at her, so that she was nearly sick. Her head nodded forward. Shirley was packing her Red Cross bag, slowly and carefully. Making sure she had all the things she needed. She'd brought her big kitchen table with her, which was helping to weigh down the landscape, and stop it blowing up at the corners, in the swirling backwash of the thunder jet.

Shirley had gone.

Emmy shouted out, but the jet, though silent, drowned out her voice with its vibrations. How could she expect her friend to help, when she'd been so nasty to her?

The table had gone. There was nothing but cold darkness, pulsing, and rustling. Very real darkness, without pity, with hard edges of pain and discomfort.

She was awake.

She felt for the rucksack, to get Normous, but then remembered, Nicola had the rucksack. And anyway, she'd forgotten to bring Normous. On purpose. In case Nicola saw him.

A dog was barking, far away.

What good was a bear-kangaroo, anyway? He couldn't help you, he couldn't save you. Like those blow-up beach fun animals. On the box it says:

THIS TOY IS NOT A LIFE-PRESERVER.

Cos it's cheap rubbish. No use in the real world.

She stood up, and set off walking, but this was only in her dream. When she came to the bridge, she found herself still sitting under the sapling.

She heard a dog, Scupper, Shirley's dog, and she heard Shirley's voice, whispering in the trees, slow

130

and quiet, and boring, and dependable, 'Our Lil, our Lil, our Lil,' talking to her rabbit; who had to have all these ailments and injuries, so Shirley could practice her bandaging.

Emmy looked down at her own paw, which was big, and bloody in the fleshless knuckles. It would have to be cut off, unless she could hide it under a bandage, or a jet's thunder.

Cold again, jagged.

She was awake.

She could tell when she was awake, because the chill bit to the bone. She looked at her hand. The paw had been cured. That was good. That was something to be grateful for. Her heart surged up with gratitude, and warmth, for Shirley, who had helped her.

She stood up, and walked to the bridge, but a bus got in the way, a big road, noisy with traffic, so she could not cross, and a rabbit, squashed in the middle of the eighth lane, not dead, still quivering. She knew she must go and help it, or put it out of its misery, but the cars whooshed past, and she didn't want to have to see the injured animal close up. Especially, she didn't want to touch it.

The darkness went black again, and the chill caressed her round the ribs, and deep under the ribs. She shuddered, and tried to get up, and she knew this was real, because it was so difficult, she was so stiff, and it all seemed pointless, much easier to get up in the dream. In a dream you can go anywhere, and you know that if it goes wrong, you'll wake up and everything is all right.

Barking.

The dog is after her. This is real, because the darkness is not spongy, it is hard edged, and cold. The only way to escape the dog is to sleep, and to dream.

She's sitting under the tree, and the sun is blinding hot, she doesn't want to get up, the sea is crashing on the shore twenty or thirty metres away, but the dog won't come close enough to let her have the barrel.

'That's cos cold drinks when you're hot are bad for you cos the shock in your tummy gives you a heart attack.'

Shirley is telling her this, sitting next to her, in her uniform, despite the heat ('in July and August we can take the tie off' – big deal!), talking, and the tears are in Emmy's eyes, because her friend hasn't deserted her, she's come to save her: true, loyal, Shirley. Emmy tries to say how grateful she is: her eyes are streaming with tears, but her lips won't move, the words, so urgent, are trapped, and can only escape in little meaningless grunts.

'Shirley,' she tries to shout, but the word is strangled in her throat, nns and mmms, like a drunk swearing on a bench in the park.

The door of the classroom is shut, and she is outside, and inside are all the others, and help, but she does not dare knock on the door, or open the door, because she knows they will all howl with laughter at her, because she has no legs.

Which is why she knows for certain that the dog

132

cannot be real. It cannot be sniffing at legs which she no longer has. Yet its bark is loud, impatient, close to her ear.

Her eyes sprang open, and her heart leapt with fear.

Inches from her face were two yellow eyes, in a head she could not see, and a mouth, breathing hot, foul air into her nostrils. For a moment, the eyes disappeared. There was another high, reckless yelp, and then the eyes reappeared. Paws were kneading into her thighs. The dog was standing on her legs. She was very stiff. At first she couldn't feel her legs, but now, as she tried to move, painful pricklings saturated the veins.

Each time she shifted, the dog scrambled back on top of her. She could make out its head, shaggy and unkempt, with drooping ears. The dog barked again, but this time its yelp did not frighten, only annoyed her, and she told it to shut up.

'Don't be so ungrateful,' said the bald girl, 'I reckon you're lucky he found you.'

20

Bus Ride

The dog's name was Tiny, and the bald girl's name was Marcia. Her boyfriend was called George, and he was mostly bald, too. His scalp was blue with tattoos, at which Emmy would have liked a closer look, but was too shy to ask.

'It's like the Tardis,' Emmy said, about the bus, where Marcia had taken her. 'It's nothing like a bus inside.'

The bus had been gutted, apart from two or three of the front seats, and fitted out like a small house. The blue-white flame of the paraffin lamp gave everything an edge, like magic. Emmy couldn't stop talking, chattering on, her breath coming in little gasps.

Marcia gave her dry clothes, and wrapped her in a blanket, which smelt doggy. Tiny sat in a corner, attentive.

'I think he's worried about me,' chattered Emmy, shuddering.

'Probably worried about his blanket,' said Marcia.

134

'Shock,' said George, poking his head round one of the partitions. 'That's why she keeps rattling on.'

'No it isn't!' objected Emmy. 'It runs in the family.'

'What – verbal diarrhoea?' said George.

They all laughed. Emmy couldn't stop laughing. She laughed and laughed, until the tears came, and then she was sobbing, and she couldn't stop crying. Tiny growled, like a warning, in his throat.

'Shut up,' said Marcia.

Tiny yelped.

'We better get her home,' said George. 'Where do you live?'

Emmy made to speak, but couldn't remember the name or the address of her new house. Instead, she smiled a smile which felt like it belonged to someone else, putty instead of lips, a Nicola-smile, and said to George: 'Let's see your head.'

Dutifully, George bent down. Emmy winced, but reached out and touched the dull blue skin. She felt strange, silly and young. She desperately wanted to show them how grown up she was. She shuddered again.

'The Lodge, Tinderford Road, Slobowen.' The address had popped into her head, and out of her mouth.

Then she was sick.

The argument that followed, between George and Marcia, seemed to take place muffled behind a screen, obscured by pinpoint lights that flashed on and off unpredictably.

Emmy sat and listened, leaning on the arm of the

chair, her head over a bucket. Marcia was saying they should drive her home in the bus. George was saying he'd much rather go on foot and ring up from the phone box, because of the petrol, and the bother of unparking the bus, and turning it, not to mention the fact that the kid would probably be sick again all over another precious rug.

'The phone box is ten minutes walk away, and anyway, we don't know the phone number, we don't know who to ring, we don't know how ill she is, the best thing is to get shot of her as fast as possible. The last thing we want is a corpse on our hands.'

Hearing that, Emmy laughed. Marcia, and George, and Tiny, looked at her. Emmy looked away. George got up, and climbed through into the driver's seat.

Embarrassed, Emmy kept her head down, looking at the carpet, and the newspaper George had spread over the patch where she'd been sick.

BOOM OR BU –

the headline read, before it got torn off.

Just behind her chair was a cardboard box, which was rustling and making small noises.

The engine of the bus coughed and sputtered, then let out a big bang like a bomb going off, and stopped. Emmy jumped. Marcia went over to the box:

'This is Tiny's latest family. Want to see?'

Emmy nodded.

The engine fired again, sputtered, ran at very low revs, so you could hear every cog and piston creaking and hissing and slapping: then stopped again.

'Takes a couple of goes to warm up,' said Marcia. She knelt down beside Emmy's chair, and pulled the box nearer, so Emmy could see inside. Tiny shuffled half a bum's length closer, sniffing.

The box was lined with what looked like old curtains. In it was a bitch with three puppies. The bitch was similar to Tiny, but smaller, with reddish fur.

'Her name's Ginge,' Marcia said.

The puppies were small, thin, and very hairy. Their heads seemed too big and old for their bodies. They fell over each other, and mewed like kittens.

'They're funny,' said Emmy. The bus kicked again, a spasm ran down its whole length. George gunned the engine, which raced for a couple of seconds, popping and whining. Then the bus relaxed. George eased off the throttle, and the bus subsided into an almost contented vibration.

Emmy reached down to touch one of the puppies, but Ginge yelped, and Tiny squeezed out a fierce growl, ending in a high bark. So she pulled her hand away. The clutch juddered, and the bus staggered forward a couple of inches, the vibrations increasing in frequency, sending odd items tumbling off shelves and tables.

'Right,' said Marcia. 'I think we're on our way.'

21

Home

Mr and Mrs Dugdale were arguing, by phone, about whether to panic or not.

Mrs Dugdale told her husband that she'd got Nicola, who'd come back.

'Come back from where?'

'By the bridge, they went off together, exploring, I've been back, she wasn't there.'

'Where's Emmy?'

'I just told you, I don't know.'

Mr Dugdale told her to keep calm. Out of his wife's jumbled account he managed to build up some sort of picture in his mind: his daughter was missing in the middle of nowhere, in rough country, in the dark, in midwinter.

'What shall I do?' Mrs Dugdale demanded, as though there must be a correct procedure, and he ought to know what it was. He opened his mouth and shut it again. He had been going to say, 'panic': but that was when the door bell rang.

He ran to answer it, hardly daring to hope, but

hoping all the same. Seeing three ragged figures on the doorstep, not to mention a big ragged dog, he was at once disappointed, scared, angry.

'Clear off,' he said. 'I'm not giving you anything.'

'We don't want anything,' the bald girl replied. 'We've got something of yours.'

Mrs Dugdale put the receiver down. She leant against the hard ridges of the booth, relief flooding her. She found she was reading the list of local dialling codes:

Tallyth

Trelton

Wortley Edge –

Irritating, silly names! Relief now ebbed, swept away by anger. What a dance she'd been led! What a waste of time and effort and torment, that she should be reading silly names in a cold phone box in the middle of nowhere at this time of night! Frowning, she pushed open the heavy door. Nicola's face, pale with anxiety, peered out at her, framed in the car window. Not like Nicola at all. Like a little frightened animal.

'She's OK, she's home already,' Mrs Dugdale snapped, getting into the car.

After that, they drove in silence for a while.

Why not? Mrs Dugdale thought. She wouldn't lose her temper, but why should she be all mumsy and mild? She didn't feel mumsy and mild. She felt hard done by.

It wasn't far to the Lodge, and Nicola wanted to

say something before they got there. She rolled the words around in her head and on her tongue, but could not bring herself to say them out loud. Emmy's mum didn't make it any easier, driving doggedly, eyes front, mouth set.

They turned onto the Tinderford road. Soon it would be too late. Nicola forced herself to speak.

'Mrs Dugdale, I took your money, I did it for a joke, I was wrong, I'm sorry, and I pushed Emmy in the water, and I've been mean to her all week, and I've been trying to get her into trouble with you just for fun, and you don't realise how much it hurts her when you're horrible to her, she's doing her best. It's not fair, if you're hateful to her now. It's my fault. It's only because she's not as clever at getting away with things as I am.'

Mrs Dugdale stopped the car. The confession itself was surprising, but even more so was the tone. She would not have believed Nicola capable of such an anguished infantile lisp.

She took a deep breath, and leaned back in the driving seat. It was a fact: for all her good intentions not to lose her temper, the anger was there, bursting to get out. If Nicola hadn't spoken, she would have marched into the Lodge, and within minutes, seconds, she would have been off. Rag lost. Scene. Pain. Blaming Emmy.

Nicola sat hunched up, peering away from Mrs Dugdale out of the window. Frankly, even while she was speaking she had disgusted herself with her own babyish tone: pathetic, yukky, weedy. But it

140

seemed to have done the trick. Mrs Dugdale touched her arm.

'Don't worry, Nic. We knew about the money. And the rest. Well, Emmy's what you call a born victim. But thank you for telling me. I know what an effort it must have been. Thank you very much.'

Marcia, and George, and Mr Dugdale sat round the kitchen table, sipping beer. Emmy, wrapped in her dad's sleeping bag, lay on the kitchen settee. Tiny sprawled in front of the Aga, watchful.

Mr Dugdale hadn't exactly invited the travellers in. Hugging Emmy on the doorstep, he was thinking about it, but also about the stains they might leave on the furniture, and the possibility of things going missing; but Tiny had made up his mind for him, sweeping past, carelessly banging against his legs, unable to resist the temptation to explore a new place. And Mr Dugdale thought: why not? After all, it was Christmas.

When he had heard the bare outline of Emmy's story (which didn't include anything about a boat), he said she must go to bed; but somehow the order never got carried out.

The talk soon moved to casual work in the neighbourhood. It turned out that George did some general building and labouring, and Mr Dugdale was eager to pick his brains.

A thought struck Emmy:

'What about Nicola?' she called out, interrupting Mr Dugdale in mid-sentence.

'She's OK. Your mum found her.' Emmy snuggled lower in the bag.

She was desperately tired, but wide awake, too. She felt sick and hungry at the same time. She nibbled some quiche. The light trailed off things when she moved her head. She wanted to make friends with Tiny. He was sprawled, a few feet away, his head propped on his paws. Several times she reached down a hand, tentative, but he growled, and she pulled away.

'He doesn't mean anything,' George said. 'It's just his way of talking.'

'He's got puppies,' Emmy said, to her Dad.

Mr Dugdale was interested at once. He started asking questions, as if he was an expert, although he knew more about fertilizer than he did about dogs.

'They're not really any particular breed,' Marcia said.

'Oh, I don't know,' said Mr Dugdale, 'I think the sire looks a bit like an Irish something, doesn't he?'

Tiny glanced over at Mr Dugdale, aloof.

'Definitely an Irish something. He's got that look. Or, at least a part Irish something.'

Emmy held her breath. She knew her dad was in a warm, generous mood, eager to make grand gestures. He swung round towards her:

'Did you like the puppies?'

She nodded.

'Would you like to have one?'

She nodded again, unable to speak. He turned back to George and Marcia, beaming.

'When children get to a certain age,' he said, 'it's very hard to find a present they really appreciate. But, it looks like we might be able to find a home for one of your pups. If there's any going spare.'

'We don't give them to just anyone,' George said.

Mr Dugdale's smile disappeared.

'We'll pay the going rate, don't worry.'

'It isn't money,' said Marcia.

'Hadn't we better ask Mum?' Emmy said.

Marcia came over and knelt by Emmy.

'Would you like to have one of Tiny's kids?'

She nodded.

'Well, they're not ready to leave their mum yet. I tell you what. You come and see them whenever you want for the next couple of weeks, and if at the end of that time you still want one ... '

'And if we still want you to have one,' George added.

'Yes, and your mum's in favour, then I don't see why we can't come to an arrangement.'

'So I can come to the bus, and visit?' Emmy asked.

'Sure,' said Marcia.

George smiled. 'I certainly don't intend driving it over here on a regular basis.'

Mr Dugdale was still a little peeved.

'I'll vouch for Emmy, you know, I'll make sure she looks after it.'

George shuffled in his chair.

'Mr Dugdale, maybe it isn't Emmy who needs the vouching.'

Mr Dugdale's mouth snapped shut, and his neck glowed red.

Marcia said they better make a move. As she and George got up, and Tiny stretched, there was the sound of a key in the front door. Emmy shut her eyes, pretended to be asleep, and waited.

'We won't mention the puppy to your mum to-night,' hissed Mr Dugdale. 'She's probably a bit distraught.'

There was a rush of cold air as the kitchen door opened, and almost immediately Emmy felt the set-tee sag, as someone sat down beside her. Her eyes still closed, she reached out a hand, which touched her mother somewhere, maybe on the shoulder or the arm. It all felt the same, the coat material. Mrs Dugdale took the hand, and kissed it.

Emmy sat up, and put her arms round her mother's neck, and clung to her, trying to find a comfortable spot for her face against the stiff mate-rial of the coat. Through her half-closed eyes, she could see Nicola seating herself, prim and inconspic-uous, on a chair in the corner.

'I'm sorry,' Emmy mumbled, her eyes shut, the dark pulsing in her head. 'I'm really, really sorry.'

'No,' whispered Mrs Dugdale, rubbing her back. 'I'm the one who's sorry.'

'And me,' called Mr Dugdale. 'If we're having a mass repentance.'

Marcia and George, already on their feet, and awkward, made their excuses.

'There's really no need to go,' said Mr Dugdale,

who wanted them to like him; but they insisted.

'Can't leave the bus blocking the road, can we?' said Marcia.

Mrs Dugdale smiled.

'I know, I know, I was wrong. I thought you were – I don't know, I was scared of you.'

Tiny barked.

'I can only say I'm sorry, and thank you very, very much.'

George ruffled Emmy's hair.

'Just don't make a habit of it. It's murder getting that bus started.'

'See you, maybe,' Marcia said.

'Definitely!' Emmy was positive.

'There's a footpath down to our lane, it runs past your garden,' George said.

'And through it in some cases,' added Marcia.

Mrs Dugdale smiled again. 'You're welcome any time,' she said.

'You can camp there, if you like,' Mr Dugdale called.

Mrs Dugdale gave her husband a quick look.

'It's OK,' said George. 'No danger of that, not at the moment.'

Emmy, with an effort, peeled herself soggily away from her mum, and turned her head, and opened her eyes.

'Thanks very much for – '

But she couldn't think of a word to describe what Marcia and George had done for her.

22

The Fish Fly Low

Next morning, Nicola asked if she could phone home. She took the phone out into the hall. Mrs Dugdale overheard her talking some nonsense about fish flying low in the tank. There was a long silence, while whichever parent it was replied, then Nicola exclaimed:

'But you promised!'

When Nicola, looking gloomy, brought the phone back into the kitchen, Mrs Dugdale asked her if there was anything the matter. Nicola shook her head.

'Because, if you wanted to go home, I'd understand.'

Nicola forced a smile. 'No! Course I don't want to go home.'

'I really wouldn't blame you, what with one thing and another.'

'No, I'm having a great time.'

Back in the bedroom, Emmy asked if she'd managed to get through.

'Yes.' Nicola laughed. 'They don't want me.

They're going off to Scotland this afternoon, for a second honeymoon.'

Silence, for a bit. Emmy sat on her bed, fiddling with Normous's ears. Nicola neatly unpacked the bag she'd neatly packed earlier on. Emmy spoke first: 'So, we're stuck with each other for Christmas?'

'Looks like it.'

'Well, the least we can do is be grown up about it.'

'What, be nasty to each other all the time?'

Emmy laughed. 'All right, be ungrownup. Be polite, and civil – '

'Pass the salt and pepper – '

'Best behaviour.'

They both smiled.

'She's all right, really, isn't she?' said Nicola.

'Who?'

'Your mum. For an invalid.'

Emmy was surprised, and pleased. Recently, she'd simply assumed that everyone found her mother unbearable.

'And I'm sorry I pushed you in the water,' said Nicola. 'But you should have seen yourself. You did look stupid, splashing about in that disgusting anorak. Hey – '

The phone was ringing. Nicola ran to the landing, hoping it was a reprieve call from her parents, but it was Shirley, wanting to know where Emmy had got to yesterday.

Shirley was hurt. It was no mean feat to get her mum to agree to her having friends round. Mrs

147

Bridle was dreadfully old fashioned, doing a set piece 'tea' with little sandwiches and sausages on sticks and fairy cakes. So, when Emmy didn't turn up, she was furious. And Shirley had taken a lot of trouble organising an interesting day, including a Games Compendium (because she knew Emmy liked board games), and mucking out horses and maybe even riding one if the woman at the stables was in a good mood.

Emmy, aware of her mum listening as she emptied the washing machine, took the phone out into the hall. 'I'm really, really sorry, I was really looking forward to it.'

Shirley asked, then why hadn't she rung to say she couldn't come?

'Look, it's a long story. I'll explain. Why don't you come over this afternoon?'

'Is Nicola still there?'

'Yes, but she's on best behaviour.'

Nickie was standing on the stairs with her hands folded like an angel.

'Oh go on, come over. Please! My dad'll fetch you.'

'Will I?' asked Mr Dugdale, as she put the phone down.

'Yes,' she replied, hugging him, and putting on a sickly voice, 'cos you're the best daddy in the world.'

'Gangway,' called Mrs Dugdale, tottering out of the kitchen with a large basket of wet washing. She walked like a tight-rope walker, as though it was fun, carrying wet washing.

'It so happens,' said Mr Dugdale, kissing his wife as she staggered past, 'that I've got to go over Shirley's way for a very secret assignment.'

'I reckon your parents are Making An Effort,' said Nicola, as they waited by the Landrover.

'Well, I wish they'd do it more often,' Emmy replied.

23

Normous on Top

They came back not only with Shirley, but with a tree.

This tree was nothing like the last one. It was neat, short, and spindly. It had a built-on ready-made stand, and a red tape tag at its crown.

'They're colour coded to show how tall they are,' explained Mr Dugdale. 'They come from Belgium.'

They'd also bought two new boxes of baubles, and several packs of tinsel, in four colours.

Emmy did most of the decorating. Nicola got distracted by an interesting article in one of the old newspapers Mr Dugdale had put under the tree. Shirley was keen to do her bit, but it took her ages, pondering where to hang each bauble. Then she agonised over whether it looked all right. And she used mainly purple tinsel. Emmy said nothing, but feared her mother's reaction.

While they decorated the tree, Emmy told Shirley about yesterday. It was hard to get things in the right order, and whenever she got to an exciting bit,

Nicola said something that made it sound stupid. Shirley, however, did not laugh. She had a First Aider's concern, especially about the soaking.

'You can get exposure, and hypothermia, and goodness knows what jobby if you're wet like that,' she said.

'I don't think she's caught a jobby,' said Nicola. 'Not Emmy. You have to be Grossops born and bred to catch a jobby.'

Emmy smiled. Shirley did not see the joke. She dropped her piece of purple tinsel, and marched over to the settee. Nicola's mouth opened, but she didn't have time to speak. Shirley grasped her by the neck of her pullover, dragged her up, and then with both hands shook her.

'A joke's, a joke, but don't, go, too, far,' she hissed. With the last word she flung Nicola back onto the settee. Nicola's mouth tried to form yet another quip, but the lips quivered, and let her down.

She sobbed.

Shirley went back to the tree. Nicola had her face buried in the arm of the chair. Emmy continued decorating.

'She doesn't really mean it,' she said to Shirley.

'If she doesn't mean it, she shouldn't say it,' Shirley snapped.

'I know,' said Nicola, muffled by the arm of the chair. 'I shouldn't say it. But I do.'

For a couple of minutes there was silence, as Emmy and Shirley worked on the tree, and Nicola lay on the settee. Then Nicola sat up, and stood up, and selected a length of gold tinsel from the box, and humbly, cautiously, looked for a place for it on the tree.

Mrs Dugdale came in. She noticed Nicola's blotchy face, but did not mention it.

'What do you think?' said Emmy, still worried about the purple tinsel.

Mrs Dugdale smiled, and said it looked 'very colourful', and only fussed a little with a few of the bits and pieces, and pushed the most prominent bits of purple out of sight behind things.

'Where's the fairy?' Nicola asked.

Emmy looked to her mum. 'We don't believe in fairies, do we?'

Mrs Dugdale laughed. 'We've never had one before.'

'Got to have a fairy,' said Shirley.

'Oh well, maybe we'll make an exception this year. Or a compromise. I think I know the very thing.'

Mrs Dugdale ran upstairs, and came down with Normous. Balancing on a chair, she set about fixing him with sellotape to the top of the tree.

The girls crowded round.

'That's not a fairy,' said Nicola.

'He's sweet,' said Shirley.

'Better than a fairy,' said Emmy.

'It'll keep him out of trouble,' said Mrs Dugdale, climbing down from the chair.

'Now go and switch the lights off, and fetch your dad.'

'Where is he?'

'Didn't you know? He's got his first ever carpentry job.'

'Doing what?'

'Fixing some loose fence planks for Mrs Thomas.'

'How much is he charging?' Nicola asked.

'Nothing,' replied Mrs Dugdale. 'But he says it's a start.'

'OK,' said Emmy, darting to the door. 'I'll fetch him. And after we've switched the lights on, then I've got something to ask you.'